SHIVA AND ARUN

P. PARIVARAJ

SHIVA AND ARUN

THE GAY MEN'S PRESS

First published 1998 by GMP Publishers Ltd,
P O Box 247, Swaffham, Norfolk PE37 8PA, England

A CIP catalogue record for this book is available from the British Library

ISBN 0 85449 265 8

Distributed in Europe by Central Books,
99 Wallis Rd, London E9 5LN

Distributed in North America by LPC/InBook,
1436 West Randolph Street, Chicago, IL 60607

Distributed in Australia by Bulldog Books,
P O Box 300, Beaconsfield, NSW 2014

Printed and bound in the EU by The Cromwell Press,
Trowbridge,Wilts, England

Author's Note

I am an Anglo-Indian, and although English is our mother tongue, it is very Indianized. The school I went to taught English as a second language, and although I grew up speaking English at home, in the streets it was usually the regional language of wherever we happened to be living.

That is a good excuse, I think anyway, to explain the odd grammar and sentence construction in parts. Anglo-Indians of my social background tend to write as we speak.

My long-time friend and confidant, P. J. (John) McCulloch, discouraged me, I believe rightfully so, from trying to make it too grammatically correct, as it would change the nuance of the way Indians, both 'pure' and 'half' castes — as many Indians see Anglo-Indians, think, speak and write in English. Perhaps I should say how we have adapted the British language into our now almost unique Indianized English.

If there is a dedication in this book, it is to John. Without his on-going encouragement I would never have even started to put down the notes of many of the 'short stories' I told him and others, as we sat on roof-tops sipping tea in the hot summer nights.

P. Parivaraj,
Andra Pradesh, 1998

Prologue: Contrasting Fates

Geet's Return

ARUN LAY still on the steel frame bed and inwardly smiled as he heard Anita's white rooster crow for the first time that morning. Not often did Arun wake up before the long red-tailed crossbreed started its morning ritual. He leaned across his cot and turned the fan off; it hadn't been hot when he went to bed late last night after marking students' papers, but the fan was one way of keeping the mosquitoes away from him. He was sure that he had mosquito-attractive blood.

Arun didn't keep a diary nor did he have a section in his mind for special events, special days, super special days, but as he breathed in several times, thinking about getting up, he thought, 'If I had to name the special-event day of the last two years, yesterday was that day.'

Had there ever been a more enlightening, more interesting, more exciting day in Arun's whole life! He didn't think so. He peeled the pink rose-printed sheet back and slowly sat up, stood, stretched and turned to look back at the bed. Two years ago when he had purchased the steel frame bed from Murty Steel Furniture And Office Supplies the salesman, not knowing the situation, had said with a smile, "It's strong enough to stand a lot of action and hard work."

Two years later the salesman's words had proved right.

Geet lay on his stomach, sleeping silently, not stirring. Arun had never closed his business in the last two years, not even when he had malaria. He had dosed himself up with chloroquin and aspirin and glucose and kept working. Today was the first day that he felt he had a reason to break the rule and hang up a CLOSED FOR THE DAY sign. Arun heard a familiar patter of feet coming along the path.

He hastily tied his lunghi and took three quick steps to the door. He beat the caller from ringing the bell. The boy was about to reach up and press it just as Arun swung the door open. Arun smiled at him. The boy looked still half asleep as he handed Arun the little two-cup thermos flask. Arun nodded and the boy half trotted down the cement path and out the gate, carrying two other flasks.

Arun took the cotton towel from the hook behind the door and walked outside. The air was fresh and crisp. He could smell the fragrance of the jasmine plant in the air. Looking at the pot plants on the verandah he realized he had forgotten to water them yesterday too.

He crossed the small courtyard and stood on the raised platform of the well, cleaning his teeth and watching the sun rise above the ashoka trees in an intense orange ball muted by thin clouds that were almost just vapour. It was going to be a hot day, he knew. He leaned over the well and saw his reflection in the clear water just a few feet down. Using the small metal bucket he filled the large clay pot with the clear cool water.

The owner of the building had said a dozen times that he would get a municipality water-pipe connection, but Arun had said no. The pipe water either smelt of a staleness he didn't care to think about, or stank of chlorine that they dumped into the supply tank.

As he squatted down to bathe, he picked up the red Lifebuoy soap. For a minute he sat here, just looking at the soap and thinking. For two years Arun had been careful with his earnings. He poured water over himself slowly with the small brass pot he used as a jug. The Lifebuoy was economical but not a very inspiring smell. Now he felt he had reason to change that and a few other things in his life. He drained the bucket and stood up wiping himself with the long cotton towel.

The words of a song came to his mind. It was a foreign song that had become popular when he was studying, and the words were often changed by the students to suit the occasion. Only one word came into his mind, 'Yesterday'.

Yesterday had started out like any other Wednesday. Students poured into his Tutorial Institute from six in the morning. The school- and college-going students came in the early morning and the private exam students came later. By one o'clock the last batch had gone off with their day's notes and homework. Arun had closed up and walked across the road to have lunch with Anil and Navjoti. By one-thirty, almost like a ritual, he was back in his bedroom and lying down to take his siesta. No matter what the students pleaded, he had got into the habit of a post-lunch siesta, and liked it. He often felt he needed it. Some of the tutorial students were slow on

8

the uptake. He had dozed off immediately.

Then suddenly he was awake. He didn't know what had awakened him. He lay there not moving, listening. No sound. Had it been one of those red-coloured ants that had bitten him? He could never find their nest or the hole where they made their exit. It seemed that never a week went by without one of them attacking him during his siesta.

No noise, no ant. He looked at the clock, two-thirty. He rolled over and went back to sleep.

Like clockwork itself though, Arun woke up fully at three-thirty sharp. He quickly put on his shirt and pulled on his jeans. No one else in a teaching position like his wore jeans. He knew that many of the students used this on their parents: "But Mr. Muddli wears jeans." He had no idea what the parents replied, but he imagined that a few at least thought, "And you want to be like him!"

He looked in the mirror, and promised himself for the thousandth time that he would buy a new and bigger one next week. He brushed his hair, wiggled his moustache, reached up and pulled the three dead incense sticks from the Nataraj print and dropped them into the cane waste-paper basket.

He breathed in deeply and walked to the door, flipping the catch back and swinging it open. He looked out and saw Miss Reenu the English tutorial teacher going into her room early. They never mixed socially, but they were good friends. They shared many thoughts on education and how the Institute should be run to ensure that the students had first-class guidance. Every now and again she would totally surprise Arun by bringing food for him from her home. If these gifts related to festivals he would have understood, but they rarely did. Her father dropped her off every morning as he went to his office and she sat marking papers for an hour every afternoon waiting for him to pick her up.

Her father never came inside the Institute, just sat on his scooter waiting for her if she was not at the gate. A few times Arun had spoken, or said simply "Good morning" or "Good afternoon", but he simply nodded, never even spoke.

Arun looked round to his right, and something moved and caught his eye. It was a young man, sitting and watching him. He sat at the end of the brick bench on the verandah, his arm resting on a large case. The young man smiled and stood up.

Arun closed the door with one hand and took a step towards him. The young man kept smiling. Arun knew the smile, a smile he had remembered many nights but not seen for more than a year.

"How are you, sir?"

"I'm well, Geet, how are you?" Arun said in reply.

They stood still looking at each other. Geet was now as tall as Arun. His hair was cut in a modern style. His face still looked boyishly fresh and you couldn't see a beard line. He had on a white shirt and the top button was undone. Arun saw his upper chest was still hairless.

"Sit down, the boy will come with tea in a minute. Tell me what you have been doing. I thought you must have forgotten me." Arun was going to say something about not even receiving a Diwali card, but let it pass.

"No sir, I have not forgotten you, not one day did I not think of you in the last year. That's why I'm here really. I finished my B.Ed. with first-class marks. Won a gold medal too. Learnt to type and did a short course on Computer basics."

He paused and looked down. He leaned a little forward and looked at Arun rather intently and smiled just ever so slightly. "I've come to be with you, sir."

Arun took that to mean he had come to ask for a job. Having a bachelor's degree in anything, including a B.Ed., was no surety of a job in India. If there is one thing that India has a surplus of, more than enough to export, it is unemployed college students with a 'B' of some kind after their name.

Geet had been a student at St. Thomas's College when Arun had been the lecturer in science and maths. He had often come to Arun's parents' home when he was living there and asked questions. Arun wasn't very keen on students doing this, simply because the questions were usually run-of-the-mill homework questions whose answers were in their textbooks. Geet's questions had always been what Arun thought of as 'extension' questions. Questions inquiring about the unusual.

Arun sat up straight, looked at Geet and without expression said, "You know that I always thought of you as a good student." A second unspoken thought flashed simultaneously across his mind — *and a sexy-looking student too.* "It was me that helped you get the seat at A.U. because I knew that you would be a serious teacher one day."

Arun waited for the tea boy to come up the path and put down two large glasses of hot tea from his wire carrying basket. The boy smiled, walked down the path and went into Miss Reenu's room.

They both sat sipping their tea in silence. Geet finished drinking and leant over and put the empty glass on the floor. As he leant over he put his hand on Arun's knee. Arun felt himself flush. The touch seem to send a tingle straight to his crotch.

"Geet, I am in need of a good tutorial teacher with your subjects and qualifications. But you know the situation. You know why I left the college. You know what I am. If you came to work here, well, people would talk. They would say something. They would say things that you might hear and that would hurt you I'm sure. When you are what I am, and you tell it —" Arun paused, breathed in, sighed — "Well there is a price to pay for honesty. It hurts when people walk by and don't acknowledge you. It hurts when you don't get invited to functions because of what you are. I don't want any of that to rub off onto you simply because you work here."

Geet looked at Arun straightly. "I didn't say that I just wanted to work here. I said that I wanted to be with you."

Arun's mind flipped. He was sure Geet was somehow mixing up the terminology. Maybe he didn't really understand the situation, the events, the changes.

Geet looked down and then back up and smiled. "I don't care what people might or might not say. I know the situation. I understand that." He stopped; a few afternoon tutorial students were coming through the gate. "I want to be with you, not just for work. In fact that's really not the point. I'm the same as you. You remember the night that I stayed with you. The night before I went to Calcutta. I was waiting and waiting for you to say something." Geet paused. "Some word. I wasn't brave enough then to say it, like I can say it now. I wanted to, but I couldn't."

Arun felt frozen, as though he was stuck in time. Perhaps this was some kind of dream, yet it couldn't be. He wondered if his brain had snapped. Geet couldn't be saying what he thought he was. He couldn't be.

"I am gay, and I have known it ever since the day I first masturbated. My fantasies were always about males, never about girls. The last year at college I would go to sleep every night having some fantasy about you. I've always wanted to be with you."

More students were coming in. Arun didn't know if he could even stand up. Geet stood up. "Can I put my case in your room?"

Arun somehow stood up, moved across the verandah and opened the door. He walked in and Geet followed, pushing the door closed. He put down the case and as Arun turned, Geet hugged him tightly, pressing their firmnesses hard against each other.

"I'll wait here, you shouldn't be late for classes."

They smiled at each other and unwound from the hug. Arun couldn't say anything. He just left the room.

* * *

Sunday afternoon, the most relaxing Sunday afternoon that Arun had spent for more than two years. The most relaxing afternoon he'd had since S.M. had suddenly left, and kind of changed his life!

The ceiling fan was on high. It was warm, even with the two upper louvre windows opened. They were lying together, legs entwined, arms around each other, not talking very much, just looking, smiling, relaxing. They had been 'doing their thing', as Geet called it. They had been doing it ever since lunch, and it was almost time for afternoon tea. Arun had enjoyed missing his afternoon siesta this Sunday!

Geet wriggled free and sat on the edge of the cot. He picked up the comb from the table and ran it through his hair. He then leaned over Arun, and combed his pubes.

"I think you would like to go into me, penetrate, wouldn't you?" Arun was running his hands over Geet's back as he spoke.

Geet didn't say anything, just went on combing.

"I like it that way, sometimes, when the feeling's right." He paused. Geet went on combing. "It's been a couple of years since I did that with anyone though." He paused again. "I would have liked to have done it that way a few times in the last couple of years. There have been three chances when I could have, but I was too scared. This AIDS thing is really frightening."

Geet stood up, walked naked across to the little bench in the corner, and started to make coffee.

"The AIDS thing really scares me too," he said. "I told you about my three-month thing with the guy from our college canteen. We really did like each other, or I really liked him. I honestly thought that he and I were..." Geet paused, finished making the coffee, turned and walked back with the mugs to the bed. "Well, I didn't think he was having it off with other blokes, and of course he was. He got caught in Pearl Park one night. There was a real stink in the college about the police raid. They caught him, two students, and one lecturer. The Head paid a pretty big bribe and got it all

12

hushed up. Narenda lost his job of course."

Geet sipped his coffee. "Honestly Arun, the way he acted, the way he let me go in, well I honestly thought that it was the first time for him too. It was for me. Now of course I realize that he was an old hand at it."

Geet stood up, still naked, walked to the end of the cot, and sat down. "I confronted him the afternoon he was leaving. He just laughed and said, 'You think that yours is the only cock that wants it the way I give it,' and he laughed and walked out. After that I never did anything with anyone until I came back here. That's honest."

He stretched and put his mug on the table. "Not that I didn't want to, but I was rather upset, and frightened. I knew that if I went with a guy and he gave me half the chance, well I would go in. That's the way I feel."

Arun lay there silently. He listened and he understood. As much as Geet had the urge, the feeling, the need to go in at times, he felt the same about being penetrated. He remembered being with S.M.; once they both got the feeling together, about going in, they couldn't stop.

"The answer is simple, we go down to Madras, get tested and wait three or four months and retest." Arun sat up and Geet stretched across and took his empty mug, smiled and asked, "Want more?"

Arun smiled and nodded. He sat watching the tall, almost totally hairless Geet making more coffee. He had blown it twice with Geet after lunch, and now, watching him standing there naked, he felt horny again. His body, his whole being constantly excited Arun. Arun also knew this was much much more than just the sheer physicality. They were starting to communicate without speaking.

"Did you ever use a condom?"

"With the guy Narenda, no. I hadn't thought about it, hadn't thought it necessary. I told you I had no idea he was being screwed in the Park all the time." Geet came back with the mugs on a plate. He had opened a packet of coconut biscuits. "After that, to be very honest, all I ever did was masturbate and think about you. And to be honest, yes I did try a condom a few times while doing that. I fantasized about using a condom and going right into you. I fantasized about you holding my balls as I went further and further in. I had the wildest dreams of you slowly rolling the rubber on and," he paused and grinned, "and just so many things, ohhh."

Arun laughed. He couldn't believe what he was hearing. But it wasn't the first time Geet had made him laugh with his funny talk. He sourly smiled to himself as he also thought of the contrast between his new partner and SM's lack of openness.

"Truth is, Arun, that I didn't ask you about going in, because I wasn't sure if you would agree to a condom, and I had decided after the Narenda thing, never to do it again without a condom."

"Fine, we go to Madras, get tested, wait four months, retest and live and play safe. During the next four months we will support the rubber industry, simple."

Arun stood up and put his mug on the bench. Geet walked over and did the same. They stood smiling and hugging each other. "I'm glad we talked this thing through, it's important."

Arun nodded.

That evening he sat by himself out on the verandah bench. Geet had gone into the bazaar for sugar and soap. He wondered about S.M., where he was, and what he was doing. Arun suddenly felt sad, because he had this gut feeling that S.M. would be too proud to ever go and buy a condom. Too self-righteous.

Geet came back late, smiling, and when Arun asked him why he was so late, and what had he bought, Geet just laughed, and Arun realized why!

Constant Reminder: The Pink Widow

JUST AS the coconut fibre-rib broom touched the bottom of the squat pot it was stored in, the bell began to ring. She let out a short quick sigh and then a longer, deeper, more exhausting one. She felt a shudder go through her body and her shoulders sag, she winced and drew her head and neck closer to her shoulders and body as if trying to hide herself. She felt the urge to screw up her toes and clench her fingers. She braced herself against the urge to let even a small tear form in her eyes. She flicked her head to one side as if to rebuke herself and blinked her eyes quickly many times. She was trying bravely to disconnect herself from the bell and its reminding horror.

The bell kept on ringing and pealing. There was an intermittence about the ringing. It came from the flow of devotees as they came in and moved forward to grab the red cord that pulled the brass hammer. They were announcing that they were there, that they had arrived. Announcing their presence to the deity they had come to propitiate with offerings.

Standing still in her room she waited. Somehow she could not move. It was the same every evening when the bell started.

Then there was a pause. It happened every evening, she knew it well. She herself had once stood in line almost daily for as long as she could remember. The pause was for two elderly sisters, both rich and rotund. They always dressed immaculately and covered themselves with every decoration their society allowed. Their gold ornaments made them look almost like rich idols themselves. Their saris were gold-threaded. Ash covered their foreheads. Their hair was oiled and bunned, the buns encased in woven jasmine-flower chains. They plodded one leg after the other up the three stone steps and shuffled forward to ring, then pause and bow as best they could to the enshrined deity. And all of this caused the pause in the bell pealing. She knew the pause and she tried to smile at it, but only tears formed. Smiles never materialized no matter how hard she tried.

The sound of a metal pot being scraped came from the kitchen and it jolted her. It made her realize again, that no matter how small her room was, no matter how drab, how isolated and lonely it and she were, no matter how desperate she felt for human warmth, from the kitchen always came food for her. It came without love, it came without much care and it came with a little fear, but food came. No one wanted to look on her, or see her face, or hear her say any word. No one even wanted to hear a polite or appreciative 'Thank you' slip from her lips.

A small trumpet sounded. It pierced her thoughts as she stood looking at the broom she had dropped into the pot. It must be full-moon day. Of course it was, she knew it but did not acknowledge it. It had no meaning to her now. The short trumpet blast was to confirm the day to the devotees. To her it simply heralded a further confirmation of her status.

She adjusted her white sari, walked out of her room and a few steps along the darkening verandah and out to the small unused courtyard. It was walled high; a mango tree grew wildly in one corner, and in the other an old gnarled neem tree was in early flower. The courtyard was once a favourite evening recluse for the women of the house. No one went there now, though, they would have to pass her door. She went there because the bell's sound was muffled by the high wall.

She sat herself on the stone bench that had worn edges from

years of previous use. She closed her eyes and tried to meditate. Not on any great god or using any secret mantra. She just meditated to close out the thoughts of her life. She knew that in her meditation no great light would break through as the sages described. She didn't desire it either. She simply wanted the empty space, the silence. Just one hour in her day not to have to constantly recognize who and what she was. One hour in which she did not have to lower her head even as the lowest-caste servant passed her.

Just one hour in which she did not have to acknowledge to everyone, that she, Radha, daughter of Sri Om Prakash Naidu, the temple trustee, the town's leading cloth merchant, member of the board of the Sri Chatterjee Women's High School — was a widow. Draped in white, draped in disgrace because everyone held in their hearts the fear that she was responsible for her husband's death.

The truth remained in her. The truth was sealed for ever, because she would never speak it and no one would want to hear it. Even if she did, they would never believe it.

I. 'A Man Who Loves Men'

Chintana

ON THE coast at the small and now unimportant village of Avalrao is a small but well cared-for temple. On its east wall is a small engraved plaque. No one knows who took the trouble to inscribe and erect it. It is said to declare in Sanskrit that a foreigner from a distant place called Marco Polo landed there in a storm.

That at least puts some historical date on the temple for those who are interested in such things. We can therefore assume that the much larger temple at Chintana is equally old, as both places are linked through ancient trade with the east. Chintana has always been famous for its cotton cloth and its now almost defunct Kalamkari cloth-printing industry. It had risen in wealth because of this trade. Temples all over South India had once sought its wall hangings. One piece hangs today in a Calcutta museum. It measures ninety feet long and forty feet wide, and no one knows how it was woven because it is a single piece.

In the big Chintana temple is a large bronze Nataraj with emerald stone eyes and rubies embedded in the fingernails. A row of pearls are worked into one wrist. It was 'discovered' by Captain John T. Trigwell, a British officer residing as engineer at the cantonment in 1843, who somehow dated it from the twelfth century of the Christian era. Every couple of years someone from the state archaeology department calls to see if it is still there.

Marco Polo or not, the Venkatramu Rao have been the Brahmin pujaris or priests at the big Chintana temple for at least as long as history records. The temple once stood in the centre of the town, but the British changed that. They built a railway line between Madras and Calcutta and the centre of commerce shifted to the east side of the line, positioned along the bank of the Shivaganga river — considered by many as holy. Today with the factories and urban sprawl it is more like a canal filled with human flotsam and smelly dead things. Bathing in it is more likely to lead to an ear infection than a blessing.

Chintana got the railway so that the British could transport raw cotton out to Calcutta and shift the abundant rice harvests to the growing colonial towns and cities. The older part of the town still retains its own dignity and its old wealthy families. The old cloth maket does less trade than the large modern market built by the municipality for its rental income. But the power behind the modern cloth market still lies with the old market merchants. The Government Hospital is on the old side of the town, much to the annoyance of the large urban population on the other side of the railway line. The railway gate is closed constantly as trains pass every hour. There has been talk of building an overhead bridge, at every election since Indira came to power.

The big Chintana temple with its four towers and the higher dome of the central sanctuary stands on two acres of land with high thick surrounding walls. The main entrance is through two massive gates, nowadays electrically lit, so big and heavy that they are only opened on special festival days — festivals that require the ancient wooden Krishna chariot to be wheeled out. People enter through the 'camel's eye' door in the right-hand side of the big gate. Its step is worn down almost four inches.

Behind the temple spread five acres of wetland rice fields. Beyond that are three acres of dry land that speculators are desperate to lay their hands on for urban land subdivision. The lands are cultivated with care, for in them is the profit of the Venkatramu Rao family over generations. Even if no devotee came to the temple for five years, one year's rice harvest would support the priest's family in high style. But devotees do come, daily in their hundreds, on festivals in their thousands.

The Venkatramu Raos live almost opposite the west wall of the temple. Right opposite their front door, in the temple wall, is a small door that gives them easy access to the temple. The house is old, large and well kept, made of Cuddahpur stone with thick double-layered tiles on the roof.

It is said that the house was built there because of a spring that keeps a large well full within five feet of the ground even in midsummer. A long verandah with carved stone pillars runs across the whole of the front. In the centre of the front wall is a double wooden door whose carved design is a replica of the temple gates. Stone benches run either side of the doors along the wall.

The double doors lead into a hall-like room that has arches through to an open courtyard with a small ablution tank in the centre. Behind this is the large, dark and impressive devotional temple reserved for the family. Though considered private, it is where some of the public come — those that are invited, rich, and seeking special pujas and blessings. Once it was only Brahmins who found their way into this private place of worship, but now it is more the size of purse than the number of threads that gets people admitted.

Off the main entrance hall is a part of the kitchen and a large dining room. And although the present senior Venkatramu Rao thinks otherwise, it is in this kitchen that ultimate power lies. He may grunt, grumble and make caustic comments. He often criticizes all of his family, but when Mrs. V. has made up her mind on something, and it does not work out as she considers fit — rice becomes sticky, visitors feel that the tea has insufficient sugar, and in ʌthe end Venkatramu Rao's specially prepared iddlis arrive cold and his bathing water is late.

By easy shifting of the old brass curd pot Mrs. V. and her scarcely less powerful daughter can observe who comes in through the front door and who goes out. History does not record how it is that the mortar is missing from between the two stones, giving this rather important view to the women, but it certainly is not new. Perhaps it is as old as the brass pot that keeps it concealed.

The house originally must have been neatly laid out, but now with each generation having added a room or altered a wall, it has become a maze of passages and small courtyards. In all there are four wells in the house, each in a separate courtyard, but only two are in regular use. The family is not as large as it was in the last century when one of the Venkatramu Raos had eleven surviving children.

Through all of this wandered Venkatramma Shivaji Nataraj Venkatramu, youngest son of the family. Only one thing impressed him about living in this big, old, cool — and so many ways respected — house. It was the fact that someone in the past had built a small courtyard with two small adjoining rooms. One wall of this courtyard ran along a narrow lane; a half-gate was fixed in it and only a thin person could pass sideways through it. Why it was so he never knew, but he had many ideas and theories. It was in this small courtyard with its sprawling neem tree that the smallest of the wells was found. Only three foot wide, it had a high stone platform and an old wooden bucket-wheel.

His elder brother, and his still childless wife with her high-pitched voice, lived in four rooms on the north side of the house.

19

His dear elder sister lived in just three rooms with her husband and two small children, but their rooms were the coolest and the largest. They also had a well and a septic toilet. The two children spent their lives between their two sets of grandparents. His brother-in-law was always taking them from one house to the other and back again, and was thus unable to keep a job. That seemed somehow to suit him.

Venkatramma Shivaji Nataraj Venkatramu — or Shiva to everyone other than his father, who called him Shivaji except when he wanted to sound more authoritarian than usual — took shelter in these two rooms whenever possible. He avoided his father and brother as much as he could, his father because he would ask questions that always seemed difficult for a young person to answer, and his brother because he treated him like a servant. He often used the excuse of being in his room to study. He was genuinely studious but not excessively so, as he didn't find learning a problem. What he would do in his room when he wasn't studying was draw — he could spend hours drawing freehand from memory. Two years ago he spent months of his spare time drawing in detail the view of the temple from the front verandah. He would walk to the verandah and observe and memorize for some minutes, then retreat and draw. The first attempt was just to get it in proportion on a double-foolscap ruled sheet. The second drawing was on a piece of quality card he purchased out of his pocket money.

He rather proudly gave it to his father on Shivaratri night, and had his pride deflated like a pricked balloon. His father looked at it for a minute or less, looked up and asked, "What's it for?" in an expressionless voice.

"I did it for you, it's the temple from the verandah."

"You think your father doesn't know that?" his brother said as he looked up at the drawing over the puree cakes with potato and ghee he was busily eating. "I can't imagine why you would spend time and money drawing the temple when we see it every day of our lives."

That brought an abrupt end to the conversation. His sister who had been serving them tiffin came round behind Shiva and looked at it. "Shiva, sign it like an artist would and give it to me, I think it's good. I'll have it."

"Sign like an artist!" his brother scoffed. His father had already left the room.

"Come on, don't just stand there with the curry bucket in your hand gawking like a crow at that waste of time and money." His brother spoke as if deliberately mimicking their father. Shanti walked back to stand in front of her brother. She leant over to ladle the curry onto the leaf plate and somehow managed that it very sloppily splashed on Govinda's freshly pressed white dhoti. Govinda said nothing, he knew better.

Shanti put the spoon back in the bucket and stood up slowly. "Crow am I, well let's see who serves you for the next week, because I won't. You may think you are a big man, but I think of you as my younger brother, and unfortunately you are not a big man, just a fat one."

Shiva rolled up the drawing and walked out.

"Sign it and give it to me, Shiva, I'll put it in my crow's nest" — Shanti had a light tone to her voice and Shiva knew she was trying to make him feel better. Unfortunately she did take it and put it in her room, where her husband let the two children colour over it with crayons. In the years ahead Shanti often thought of the drawing and lamented bitterly that she no longer had it.

Shanti was more than a sister to Shiva, and more than a friend — she was his confidant. He not only told her things that made her blush, but asked her those things too. She always remembered the day they were together grinding groundnuts for some festival or other. She had to make hundreds of the little cakes for the temple puja. Their mother was ill; Shiva was the only spare person to help her, or more to the point, willing to.

"You know what I read in my friend Samuel's biology book? It is the man's sperm that decides if you are born a girl or a boy. So every time that father scolds mother about you being the first-born and being a girl, well it's his fault not hers. I'm going to tell him that one day when he is saying such nonsense to mother."

"You know that the devotees of Kali used to sacrifice people, don't you?" Shanti kept on grinding the groundnuts as she spoke. "Well I wouldn't tell father what you just told me, he may install Kali as the favourite goddess in the temple and you will be the inaugurating sacrifice."

Shiva picked up a handful of nuts and sprinkled them into Shanti's hair. They sat and laughed together. Laughter was not a common sound in their house. In a lowered voice she asked, "What did you think about getting a bicycle last week?"

"I like the bicycle but I don't like the motive behind it. He only gave it so that I would think it was easy to ride to that dumb

Sanskrit school. He can't really believe that I don't want to go there. He can't really think I want to be a pujari like him and Govinda, surely?"

Shiva had stopped feeding the nuts into the mouth of the upper grinding stone.

"Really." Shanti mimicked Shiva and they both laughed. She nudged him to get on with the grinding. "Mother wants you to go to a proper college, I know that." She paused and looked around. "And you can be sure that your brother wants you to go too. He doesn't want you in the temple and getting any of the cream that he gets."

Shiva already knew only too well his brother's mentality. Two years ago their uncle had returned to take up a position rightfully his. To that nothing could be said. But his uncle had asked for the house next door. It belonged to their father but it had been rented out for years and the income had somehow found its way into Govinda's pocket. For almost a year Govinda was furious and ill-tempered at the end of each month. Each time he normally collected the rent, he imagined he was somehow being cheated by his uncle, who he hardly ever spoke to. It certainly didn't seem to perturb the uncle.

It was hot outside though only the beginning of summer. Shiva had passed his exams, he knew that. He also knew that somehow he would get to college, but in the Venkatramu house nothing was settled until it had happened and was already history. This had been the only thing that had stopped him throwing a 'fever' fit or anything that would have got him out of last week's three-day visit to Tirupati. They had all gone. It was hot there too, overcrowded and rushed. They had no preference rating there. They were just like thousands of other Brahmins in a line with innumerable other devotees.

He sat in his room and picked up the mirror. He ran his hand over his hair — well what was left of it. They had all gone through the ritual of having their heads shaved: father, mother, sister, brothers, in-laws, grandchildren — everyone. Shiva let out a sigh that was close to a groan. It would be ridiculously short when college started. But until the college thing was settled he would do whatever was instructed. He would be at every Monday night's bhajan session on the temple verandah. He would somehow suffer the yelping, out of tune, fat farmers' wives who made Monday their special day to disturb the deities with their performance. At least they were only stone and didn't have ears, and they should also be thankful that they didn't have noses. He had counted by smell five farts last Monday evening. But suffer he would. He would be there every morning to ring the bell in the sanctuary. He would cover his forehead with whatever powder was in vogue for the week. He looked in the mirror again and grimaced. Even with his hair growing normal and not too fashionably cut, he still looked very boyish.

He didn't want to look boyish going to college, but this hair-shaving had made him even more so. He ran his hands down his legs, which were covered in short fine hairs. He had watched them grow in the last year. He drew his hands up between his legs. He sat upright a little and slid his left hand down inside his shorts, running his fingers in and out of the thick mass of pubic hair. "Enough hair for a sparrow to make a nest in," he said quietly to himself, and then smiled as he thought, *At least a small sparrow with a small nest.*

He felt his cock getting hard and squeezed it slightly. Yes, he wasn't boyish any more really, he was, he thought, mature.

Wednesday

SHIVA COULD not resist the temptation to look at his father's Hindu calendar and see if this Wednesday was in their reckoning an auspicious day. He looked at the various signs and saw that it was just a plain day. A day on which one could, if one's chart was right, be married. But he certainly was not planning to get married.

Never on a Wednesday had so much happened. It all kept tumbling through his mind. He had willingly agreed to go to puja with his father and help perform the lamp-lighting ceremony. He made no attempt to escape the bhajans afterwards either. There were times when he would rebel against his father's bullying him into going to the temple to perform rituals he didn't understand. The bullying usually goaded him into making a remark that he soon regretted. His remarks always seemed to lead to a 'rudeness fine', and with such a small allowance of pocket money, any deduction hurt. He often felt that the remarks he was goaded into making cost more than they were worth, and wondered at his stupidity for falling into the trap so often.

But today, this very special Wednesday, he restrained himself completely and held his tongue in check. He sat through the whole temple bhajan session with a calm and serene face, not looking the least bit bored. His mind wasn't there at all, in fact. His mind was six hours' away at his aunt's house. He could scarcely believe that with the afternoon's post had come a letter from his aunt requesting her brother to send 'dear Shivaji to come and stay with me while I go to the special bhajan and discourses of Swami Naidu Krishna Venkatswamy from the Krishna Mutt in Calcutta. I do need his help during this time. . . '

In the morning Shiva had been helping his brother pick out caked-on turmeric and sandlewood paste from the front-door carvings. The pastes were put on the door once a week and every few months had to be picked off carefully so as not to damage the carvings. He heard the postman's bicycle bell, familiar to everyone in the street, make a dull clung-clung. The postman had a bundle of letters tied up with a string. He pulled the top six out and was about to hand them to Govinda when their mother came out. "How's your daughter today Bhaskarao, I saw your wife last night and she said she was still recovering."

Shanti now apppeared with a glass of buttermilk and a large fried sesame cake on a small plate. Bhaskarao handed the letters to their mother and sat on the step and smiled as he accepted the glass and plate from Shanti. He put them down and shrugged his shoulders.

"She is a little better but the birth was dangerous. I was so worried that she might not even live. I told her and that husband of hers not to have children so close to each other." He looked up and smiled. "The little boy is well though — poor thing, he has my nose."

He took hold of his rather large bulbous nose and wiggled it with his thumb and index finger. He laughed and they all laughed with him. He drank the buttermilk and ate the cake, and smiled and thanked them. He pushed his bicycle down to Mr. Murthy's Bookstore where he certainly wouldn't get more than a grunt from the old man. Shiva watched his mother put the letters on the large wooden swing bench in the middle of the front hall.

"Bring a toothbrush and clean these places," his brother said bossily, pointing to the top corner of the panels. Shiva walked slowly into the front hall and as he passed the swing bench flicked the letters just a little. There was one with the college stamp on it. He kept going. He dare not pick it up or touch it. A letter from the college. It could only mean he had been accepted. He was filled with unbelievable joy. He had been going to get his brother's own toothbrush to clean the door panels. He felt so good that he walked right through to the back cleaning area and found an old one. He walked back through the kitchen. His mother was smiling and Shanti gave him a smile. They had seen the letter too.

His father came in, all neatly dressed after having his second bath of the morning. He was in full civilian regalia — white dhoti crisply starched and pressed, white short shawl with its gold thread ends, an exactly correct proportioned Shiva trident painted on his forehead over very neatly spread lines of white ash. He walked round the room once with his hands folded, then stopped at the large framed print of Vishnu and lit three incense sticks which he took from a packet on the wall. He bowed and prayed and wedged the smoking incense sticks into the picture frame. Govinda had stopped cleaning the door and Shiva was scarcely pretending to be cleaning it. He was watching his father's movements.

It was a full fifteen minutes until his father sat down on the swing bench. He had put sandlewood paste on the corners of two other deities' frames, and lit incense and put the lighted sticks into the frames of four more. He sat with his legs swinging for a few minutes just watching Shiva cleaning the panels. Slowly he lifted his legs and crossed them carefully so as not to crease his fresh clothing. Shiva watched his mother come in with a small tray that she placed on her husband's lap. She had stopped the bench swinging for him. Shanti came in with a small brass pot of water and a large glass already full.

Shiva timed it so that he brushed the door and finished while the breakfast ritual proceeded. On the verandah was a large clay pot that was always filled daily with ablution water. The ladle hung on the pot's lip. Shiva stood looking down the street and washed his hands into the drain. He shook them dry and walked inside. His father had started to slit the envelopes open. The system was always to place them on one side of the bench and then read them one by one. Shiva took the morning newspaper from the stool and sat on the floor in the centre of the room in front of his father. Eventually, by the time he had turned to page 5, his father got to the college letter.

"I heard yesterday that you could get a scholarship to study Sanskrit. With your bicycle it's not too far to ride."

Shiva told himself to be calm and not be goaded into saying anything he would regret. He looked at his father. "Even with a scholarship I would not do well at the studies because I'm not really interested in that kind of subject."

He lowered his eyes as his father stared at him. He knew he had to be careful with his words. He didn't really want to upset his father, nor did he want to be forced into doing a course he was not at all interested in. How could he tell his father the truth? The truth was that he wanted to get to college as the first step out of this house, away from his father's domination. He wanted to draw plans and models of machines, even electrical things. He wanted to be some kind of draughtsman. He was not sure what it really entailed. Getting to college and studying science group was his first step, his only chance to move on and out, away from this life and house ruled by ritual. He looked up and his father was still staring at him blankly. He had moved a little on the bench and the chains were squeaking just a bit as it swung back and forth very slowly. Then his father did a most unusual thing. He flicked the envelope and two pages to Shiva, who grabbed them as they came towards him. The smell of heated oil and frying eggplant came into the room. He loved that smell and his stomach quivered.

"You have been accepted into St. Thomas's College. Just try and remember that this is not what I want for you. It's really beyond my comprehension, to want to leave the centuries of service and tradition that our caste represents. How anyone would want to study for the sake of useless knowledge when we have all we need in our lives through our worship and service, I just don't know." He paused and leaned forward slightly. The bench swung back more.

Behind his father were two lines of frames, one above the other. The bottom line was of their ancestors, all framed in black. Some were oil paintings, others watercolours. The one of his grandfather was the only photograph type and it had been hand-coloured. The second line of frames above these were prints of various deities, all different sizes, and the frames all different colours. Some looked very faded. Shiva saw that the incense sticks in the Ganesh frame were still burning. His father's bald head was moving across the painting of his great-grandfather and then up slightly, so it appeared that the centre of his bald spot was touching the feet of the enthroned Ganesh. It looked very funny to Shiva and he tried not to smile. His father kept staring at him.

"You know that I had to ask several friends for favours to make sure you got that admission. I don't like asking favours. I also had to pay more than you can imagine. Too much, I feel. But you have what you want. You are young. Just remember that now you are putting our family name in the public by going to this college. Don't bring me shame. Don't get involved in things that make problems. Don't bring any of your radical political banners or friends here."

He paused, looked around and said in a quieter tone, "Don't, don't get involved with any girls. Think always of your mother and sister."

Shiva knew that his father was about to start a long lecture. He knew he would have to sit patiently and listen and nod.

A shuffling came from the front verandah. His father looked up and slid off the swinging bench with remarkable speed. He moved quickly to the door and ushered in an old Brahmin scholar from the Sanskrit school. Shiva knew this was the time to leave. His brother, who had been sitting on the other side smugly listening to Shiva getting a lecture, got up and slipped out through the archway. His sister sat smiling at him as he crossed the room. She stopped peeling the garlic pods and clapped her hands quickly. "Congratulations, you got it. Don't let him put you off, your marks got you in. He only oiled the application a bit. And you know he will get the oil back too one day."

She stood up and reached for a Postman tin. She pulled the lid off and took out a coconut sugar sweet. "Open your mouth."

He smiled and stepped closer. She popped the sweet into his mouth. " A little kitchen prasadam for you."

He folded his hands, smiled and whispered, "Namaste."

She laughed quietly and sat down again.

"I'm going out the back way. I want to go and see Samuel and see if he got accepted. I'm sure he did."

She nodded and beckoned him to her. "Keep going to the temple with him this week and hold your tongue."

Shiva said expressionlessly, "Go to the temple with Samuel, are you mad, he's Christian."

Shanti stopped peeling the garlic again. "You idiot, not Samuel, your father."

"Ohhh," and he laughed as he saw his remark had caught Shanti out.

"Get out, idiot."

Shiva wheeled his bicycle down the side lane and rode across the Municipality Market square to the Christian quarter. There were people everywhere and it took him ages to weave in and out of the vendors. Samuel's house was behind the old Lutheran church. It was a small mud-brick building with a palm-leaf roof. Samuel's mother was a friendly woman and always made Shiva welcome. It was hard to escape from her without accepting tea and something to eat. She always scolded him for being 'so thin'.

He rang the bicycle bell and Sam rushed out of the side room where he slept and studied. "Hey, can you believe it, I got a scholarship, I got it. I can't believe it. What about you, have you heard anything?"

Shiva let the bicycle fall and ran over to Sam and hugged him. "Congratulations, a scholarship, that's great news."

Samuel's mother came out smiling. "And you Shiva, you must have got in with such good marks."

An hour passed with the three of them sitting on the verandah on stools chattering about the college acceptances. Samuel's older brother joined them. Their mother went in twice and made them lemon squashes. She sent a servant girl to get two green coconuts. Samuel's brother pierced them and they shared the coconut milk.

Samuel's mother was a Home Science teacher at the girls' high school. She was pleased for Shiva but the joy of Samuel getting a scholarship just flowed out all the time in her conversation. Shiva knew that without a scholarship they could not have managed. Samuel's father was a total drunkard. The eldest daughter was married with three children and an unemployed, unemployable husband. The salary of Samuel's mother covered the whole family. The municipality siren sounded one o'clock.

The two boys walked down the lane together, Sam wheeling Shiva's bike for him. "I'm really pleased we are both accepted Sam, I really am happy that you got the scholarship. I know it means everything to you. I'm just happy that I could get in and escape a little. I feel so caught up with my father's pressure. This is a real break for me."

Shiva stopped and grabbed the handlebars of the bike, making Sam turn abruptly towards him. "Sam, I really envy you and your family. I know you think different, but you are so free."

Sam smiled. He knew that somehow, even with their ongoing money problems in the house, he was free compared to Shiva who always seemed caught up with doing what was considered right by his father.

"Guess what? I got three weeks' work starting tomorrow. Old Gupta called me into the bookshop to help him unpack the new schoolbooks. Usual long hours low pay, but I don't care. At least

I'll have some pocket money to start college. Maybe he'll even let me have the damaged books like he did last year. Let's try and meet Saturday evening at the Clock Tower."

"Hey that's great Sam, sure, see you Saturday."

Shiva rode slowly back home through the market. He walked through the side door and along to his room. He lay down and daydreamed and fell asleep. He woke to hear his mother calling him from the main courtyard. He jumped up and put his shirt on and hurried to the front room. His sister was sitting on the floor combing her hair and rubbing oil into the strands. His mother was distributing tea to his father and brother and his brother-in-law who had just come from his parents' house. The children hadn't come back as planned and arranged. Shanti was angry, he could tell.

"I suppose now that you are going to college you'll be too busy next week to help your family clean the Lingam room."

The question was casual. Shiva had crossed the room and was sitting with his back to the the front door. The breeze was blowing nicely on his back. He felt the wind blow under his shirt, and it billowed the cloth. The Lingam room was at the east side of the temple and only used three times a year for major pujas. It took days to clean all of the stones and polish the hanging brass bells. There were literally hundreds of them hanging from lines of beams. They all had to be taken down, cleaned with the astringent juice of the tamarind fruit, polished. When polished and dry it then took hours to fit new threads to the gongs and rehang them in order. His father's question definitely had a barb to it. Shiva looked across at his brother who had a smirk on his face.

"If you tell me to do it I'll do it," Shiva replied.

His brother shuffled his feet and said to no one in particular, "Ahh, you see, that's a typical smart college student's answer already. If you *tell* me — not if you *ask* me."

His brother seemed aggressive for some reason.

"Either way, if Father asks me to do it I'll do it, why shouldn't I?"

"And as our children are still over at your parents' house you'll be able to help also for a change." Shanti almost spat the words at her husband.

"Well Shiva you have escaped from the task. My sister has sent an Inland Cover to say she would like you to go and stay with her for two weeks. She is dutifully going to hear some discourses by a renowned swami. She wants you to be in the house for her." Surprisingly his father said the last sentence with a smile.

"As the children are not here, I don't see why I couldn't go and stay with her. I like her, she's understanding. I have nothing to keep me here. Yes, why don't I go?" Shanti said this with defiance, tugging the comb through her hair. Their mother sat on the floor pretending to be engrossed in unwinding white thread into lengths.

"Shanti, I'm telling your husband now that he better get off his lazy backside and bring the children back here by tomorrow night. I'm tired of this stupid game with children. And he had better get ready to help clean the Lingam room too — and you." He addressed the last two words to Shiva's brother.

There was a hushed silence. Their father hardly ever spoke as angrily as this. He always spoke with a poke and a stick, but this was really fierce. His son-in-law got up and walked out through the arch saying nothing. Shanti got up and followed. A few minutes later everyone could hear them arguing in their room.

"Shiva, you will go on Monday morning. He must be there a day early so as not to inconvenience my sister. Get yourself organised. Get money from your mother too for travelling. And make sure you take sufficient food preparations with you."

Shiva almost felt it before he heard it. His mother chuckling: "You telling me indirectly that I need reminding to send your sister food preparations from this house, and also always pay from my pocket. Have you ever heard your sister complain about the way I treat or give her respect? Not likely. Have you ever given money to her when we know she is in need? Never. What nonsense you speak sometimes. I should send him with just enough money to get there and no food preparations, then what would she would think and say to you? Then I would listen to how you would speak to her. And... " She stopped, running out of words and steam.

Shiva ate the last of the puri on the plate and said nothing. His father sat still. She looked at him and he looked back. "Bring some decent tomato chutney for these puri woman, how many times over how many years of marriage must I remind you that I like tomato chutney only with this dish? Maybe I should get my sister to come and live here, she at least would remember. After all these years of marriage and you forget to care for me like this."

Shiva watched his mother put down the thread with a show of displeasure, but she was smiling too. "Yes, good idea, get your sister to come and stay here, she would remind you of just how rude and selfish you are."

Shiva didn't understand them. They both laughed with each other. She came back and tapped a large spoon of chutney on his plate. She then sat in front of him and they leant close to each other; he whispered something to her and she made a grunt and laughed.

"Well, what are you sitting there for watching us like a stupid monkey?"

Shiva jumped up and went out followed by his brother. They didn't speak as they crossed the yard.

Shiva felt elated. What a magic Wednesday.

Acceptance to college — "the ticket of escape" he called it — even though it was only going to a local college and still being at home, it was somehow a freedom even if he did not yet fully understand it. He was elated that his friend Sam, who made no judgements on others, would be going too. The bonus, unbelievable, was a chance to go and stay with his aunt.

He turned back from walking towards his room, and went into the family temple room. He wanted to make some kind of expression. He went over to the Nataraj oil lamp that was his own. It had been given to him by his grandmother at his birth. Someone had lit it every day of his childhood. He added oil to it and adjusted the cotton wick over the edge. He drained the surplus oil from the tray back into the stand, lit a large number of incense sticks and placed them each in the holder carefully. He stood with folded hands. No prayer or anything, just standing silent, almost inwardly, awed by everything that had happened that day. He looked up at the thick wood rafter on the low sanctuary ceiling. He walked to the stone Nandi bull, took a pinch of the red powder from the bowl and dabbed it on his forehead, then dabbed the wooden beam above the idol. As he walked out he ran his hand down the bull's cold stone back. He turned around and looked at his oil lamp. The thread flared a little and a shadow of the dancing Nataraj sprang across the back wall. He smiled. He too was somehow dancing inside himself.

That evening he lay on his bed, tired and excited, listening to the fan turning slowly. Listening to the little gecko lizards on the ceiling. He lay there thinking about the day. His thoughts were random for a while and then he started to think and imagine the stay at his aunt's house. He knew it would happen, he wanted it to happen. His penis got hard. He undid the buttons on his shorts and slowly masturbated himself. He did it slowly because there was so much to fantasise about. Then he came to the point where he couldn't stop and couldn't slow down. He called this the 'execution point'. Even if an executioner walked in he could not stop at that point. He felt his legs go taut and his feet stretched and his toes curled and he seemed to be in a void all of a sudden.

The semen flashed in three quick successive pulses up and out and across his stomach. He lay motionless. The fan whirred on. He felt some of the globules trickling down his side. He knew that he had locked the door. He turned over and felt the wet spot on the bedsheet and went to sleep.

Ramu: The Night Cobra

I T TOOK his brother-in-law all Thursday to get organised to leave and pick up the children. He eventually left on Friday and on Saturday he returned with them. The house had a certain expectation about it. Shanti was in high spirits. The children rushed into the house ahead of their father and the turmoil began. It went on for several hours. During all this Shiva managed to make contact with his brother-in-law's cousin Ramu who had arrived with him, and put his bag in the spare room in the same passage as his own room.

Ramu had finished his B.Com. degree successfully and was trying constantly to get an office job anywhere. He had sat for three bank exams but got nowhere. Being high-caste today had its distinct employment problems. Ramu was now on his way to Hyderabad for an entrance exam to apply for a position in the Corot company. They had a big factory here and another in Madras. Shiva had been to the factory here with Sam once; Sam had a cousin there who was an engineer. Ramu was hoping that he might get an office job in either Vizag or here because they were expanding into exports. There had been an ad in the newspaper and Ramu had applied and got through the first interview test. He wanted to get a letter of reference from Shiva's father. The interview in Hyderabad was on Tuesday and he would leave on Monday morning.

Shiva told him that he too was leaving Monday morning, but in the opposite direction to go and stay with his aunt. Shiva hadn't seen Ramu for almost three years. "Do you still play cricket?" he asked Ramu.

"No, last year at the beginning of the season I broke a small bone in my foot and was in plaster for six weeks. I decided that I wouldn't play again. It was just too painful to repeat. The doctor said that I shouldn't even attempt to play for two years. It was complicated, don't ask me why. He explained it and I just accepted it. I still follow it though. I umpired a match at the end of season. That was fun. And you?"

Shiva heard the five o'clock siren. He had planned to meet Sam at six at the clock tower. He was hoping that Sam and he might be able to go to the first cinema show. He was standing pulling water from the well in 'his' courtyard. Ramu was taking a bath, and Shiva was pouring water over him. He wondered if Ramu wanted to go to the cinema, or maybe he would go to puja at the temple.

"Yes," Shiva replied, "I'm still playing. In fact our famous All-India Super XI are playing tomorrow in a match against the Studs over at the Nehru Park." Shiva paused as he hooked the rope over the pulley wheel. "Want to come and watch, maybe they will need an umpire."

Ramu looked up through a soapy face. "Sure, at least I'll come and watch and cheer you on."

Shiva poured more water over him. "I'm not sure but I might be going to the cinema tonight with a school friend. It's a Kapoor film. You want to come, if we go?"

Ramu nodded as he rubbed soap once more over his head. "Wow, it was a dusty bus ride today, so hot too."

Shiva was enjoying pulling the water up and pouring it as Ramu wanted it over him. Shiva couldn't remember being so fascinated with looking at anyone bathe for almost two years. He got really turned on watching or bathing with another guy. Ramu had what Shiva called the 'dream body'. Soft hair all over, not thick and coarse, but thick and fine. Ramu had on a pair of Binny shorts that were tight enough to show his complete contours when the water was soaking through them. Shiva always liked to look at guy's pubics coming up above his shorts line. Ramu had what Shiva thought of as the 'classic' pubic hair-line — in his mind he had all hair-lines classified. Ramu looked up to get more water poured over him. Shiva had been daydreaming and hadn't noticed that Ramu wanted to wash the soap out of his hair. Ramu also had a T-line of chest hair that fanned out evenly. He hadn't shaved for a day or maybe two and it brought out the strength of his jaw. His moustache had been neatly trimmed.

When Ramu had finished bathing Shiva moved to the side of the well and sat on a small stone bench. Ramu took the cotton towel from Shiva and slowly rubbed his body dry, before rubbing his hair more vigorously. He looked up at Shiva who was just gazing at him. They hadn't spoken for a few minutes. Shiva smiled, Ramu smiled back. Shiva was sure that the 'contour' in Ramu's shorts was bigger, and maybe, maybe even a little hard.

Ramu stood facing Shiva, and quickly looked around. He pulled his shorts down and wrapped the towel around himself. But he did it slowly and looked at Shiva as he did. It was bigger than earlier, and it was a bit hard; Shiva quickly looked and noticed.

"What do you call it?" he said nodding towards it.

"Ramu's Night Cobra," Ramu said as he looked down at it and laughed.

Shiva thought it was a great name and laughed with him.

"What do you call yours, Temple Temptation or Puja Python"?

Shiva sat and said the two names over again to himself. He laughed again. "Actually I haven't really thought of a name for it. I should do."

Ramu stood and rewrapped the towel; the object of interest flashed into Shiva's view again, and it was definitely harder. There was a real bulge under the towel now. Shiva was almost glad he was sitting down, because he could feel himself getting very tight and hard.

"Okay, I'll give it a name for you tonight." Ramu smiled and winked at him. Shiva felt himself flush.

The two children came running down the corridor calling out to Shiva.

"Come and play uncle Shiva. We have a new ball."

Shiva went out with them to the front verandah and they played 'drop' until they were called for bathing. They went inside with a promise from their mother to play again later.

Ramu and Shiva went through the kitchen and out by the side gate. Ramu said he would prefer to walk than go on the bicycle. At the Clock Tower Shiva couldn't see Sam so they walked up to the bookshop where he might be working. Shiva saw him stacking books up on the top shelf. He waited for him to come down and Sam made a sign that he wouldn't be finished until too late to go to even the second show. Shiva and Ramu walked down to the Geetha Theatre. There were lines waiting for tickets at all windows. They got on the Rs 3.50 line.

Throughout the film Ramu kept his leg close to Shiva's and

quite often rubbed it against his cousin's. Shiva wasn't sure if it was anything, or maybe — maybe — a sign. It confused Shiva, and constantly made him hard.

At intermission Shiva met Sreenu and Laxman and Ramana who were all in the All-India Super XI. Shiva introduced Ramu and they talked about the film and next day's match and about going to college. Sreenu had got accepted into the engineering college at Hyderabad. That was really news. They all knew his father must have paid a small fortune for it. Laxman was still waiting to see if he would get a scholarship, and Ramana had got on to the B.A. course at the same college as Shiva.

They met again after the film ended and walked down to the Clock Tower where they found Sam waiting for them. Sreenu ordered them a cold Limca drink each to celebrate his luck in getting the engineering place.

Sam was in a foul mood; he had to work tomorrow unpacking crates of new textbooks and sorting them out. "Still, I need the money so I can't complain too much." He shrugged his shoulders. "But I did want to play tomorrow — just to see the Studs drop their balls."

They moved off laughing at his comments. Laxman, Ramu and Shiva decided to walk home the long way via the flower market. Laxman had to get jasmine flowers for his mother and sister.

Everyone was sitting on the front verandah when Shiva and Ramu reached home. The grandchildren were still up and playing. "Well the two Kapoor film experts are home. Let's eat, I'm hungry," said Shanti, leaning on her mother's shoulder as she stood up. "Was the film good?"

Ramu gave a five-minute commentary on it and made everyone laugh at his mimics.

"Your friend Abdullah came by and said to tell you that the match is starting at ten and they are going to practise at nine," Shiva's mother called from the kitchen.

"I've put your cot against the wall Shivaji, and put down two mattresses and sheets in your room for you and Ramu," Shanti said as she filled their glasses with buttermilk. She stood up and looked down at Shiva. "Don't say I don't look after you properly. I hope aunt takes as good care of you. I could still go with you if you wanted me too."

Their father clucked and Shanti caught his glance to understand that she had said enough on the subject.

Ramu and Shiva walked through the corridor to Shiva's room.

Ramu took a lunghi from his case and Shiva hung his trousers on the hook by the door.

"Is there any drinking water Shiva?" Ramu asked.

Shiva looked surprised as he pointed to the corner and saw that the small clay pot and glass weren't there. "Fantastic Shanti must have taken it and forgotten to bring it back. I won't be a minute."

When he came back with the pot and glass and opened the door, the lamp was already off and in the light coming in from the street Shiva saw that Ramu was already lying down. He put the pot in the corner on the straw ring. He had also seen what Ramu was doing. In fact he nearly dropped the pot when he opened the door. Shiva lay down.

"If you were a snake charmer Shiva you could work on this night cobra of mine."

Shiva felt light-headed. He turned on his side and with almost trembling excitement stretched out his hand; he took hold of the long thick 'night cobra' and pulled its hood back slowly. Its head was bigger than he ever imagined anyone's could be.

Ramu had slid his hand across the mattress and was undoing the button on Shiva's shorts. It was a fantasy come true. Shiva often thought of someone slowly undoing his buttons and sliding their hand inside his shorts. Now it was actually happening. Ramu took hold of it firmly and squeezed. Then with both hands he slid Shiva's shorts down and over his knees and off.

Ramu let Shiva do whatever he wanted; Shiva felt an inner joy and happiness the whole time. He ran his hands all over Ramu, tightly up between his legs and pressing into his crotch. He massaged the two large snake's eggs. He drew the hood right back and then stretched it up and drew it tight. He ran his hands up and down Ramu's hair-line and played with the hair on his chest.

Ramu drew him close and slowly blew air into his ear. This feeling in his ear while his penis was being firmly stroked nearly drove Shiva crazy. Then Shiva felt the 'executioner' coming. He ejaculated in three pulsating blows. The first felt like a thunderclap, and landed on Ramu's chest, the second and third went on his own stomach. Ramu ran his hand down Shiva's belly and wiped the warm fluid over his still very hard penis. The sensation made Shiva squirm and he grabbed Ramu's hand to stop.

"I think we should call it your 'sticky wicket' — that seems appropriate doesn't it?"

Shiva was too excited to comment. He just lay there. Two years!

Two years since he had felt as high and excited and fulfilled as he did right then.

Ramu got up on his knees, squatted over Shiva and started to masturbate himself. Shiva felt good to have Ramu crouched over him like that. He stretched his hand down to feel Ramu's balls and gently massaged them.

"Keep doing that, it's beautiful," Ramu said in a dry voice. Shiva felt Ramu's legs tighten and squeeze him. Ramu made a deep groaning sound and semen surged out and onto Shiva's 'sparrow's nest'. Ramu then leaned forward and lay on Shiva. He lifted his cousin up, wrapped his arms around him and hugged him gently. Shiva hugged him back.

A lorry went by on the front road and tooted; a dog yelped. The sound seemed to break their spell.

Ramu rolled off Shiva and said, "Now I need that glass of water." He drank it straight down.

"You really are lucky having two rooms and a little courtyard with a well like this," Ramu said this as they stood washing themselves quietly.

"I suppose so, but it's not much use if I never have a purpose for it like now!" he said lightheartedly.

"Don't tell me you have never done this kind of thing before with any of your friends?"

It was said as though Ramu didn't or wouldn't believe him if he said "no".

"It's two years since I had it like this. I mean I do it myself always, but it's two years since I did it with another guy." Shiva paused and sighed, "Two long years."

Ramu looked at him as he dried himself. "Then I suppose I'm lucky because I never go more than a month without having it like we did." He paused. "And more sometimes."

"More times than once a month, or more action than we did?"

Ramu took a small step closer to Shiva and with one hand took hold of Shiva's chin and gave him a quick kiss. As he did that he rubbed his other hand over Shiva's sparrow's nest. Shiva felt a sensation starting again.

They went inside and lay down.

"Tell me about your friend?" Shiva asked quietly.

"Well about two years ago I was in the house by myself one evening. Everyone had gone to the first show to see the latest Bachhan film release. I'd already seen it in the afternoon. It was during the monsoon. The guy who brings the milk arrived absolutely soaked. It was lightning and thunder and really heavy rain. He usually comes around the back but he ran onto the front verandah. He slipped and spilt half the milk and cut his knee on the doorstep. I took what milk there was and put it in the kitchen and brought a towel out to him. He took his clothing off and wiped himself and wrapped the towel around his waist. I said I'd get a piece of cloth for the cut. The power had gone off. I found matches and lit a candle in the middle room. I tore a bit of cloth off an old lunghi. He had stepped inside and closed the door so that the rain didn't blow in. Really Shiv, honest, as I knelt down to wipe the blood off the cut and tie the cloth, I was sure he had a hard under the towel. But it was quite dark. I had the candle on a shelf in the middle room because it would have blown out with the draught in the front room where we were. Lightning kept flashing and making some light in the room. So I bandaged the cut and as I stood up I purposely brushed him across the front of the towel. It was so hard. As soon as I touched it he immediately took hold of me too. By comparison I tell you mine is small."

Shiva chuckled. "Bigger than yours, I don't believe it!"

"Really, it is. Anyway after that as often as no one is in the house when he comes we get together. Want to hear something even more interesting?"

Shiva was feeling excited again. "Yes, of course I do."

"Well one evening I told him I was sure that tomorrow night no one would be home. First show cinema story. So I heard the knock on the door and knew it was him. I heard the milk pot being put on the step. I only had my shorts on, and I was very hard. I opened the door and there he was, but with another guy. This other guy was one of those big thick muscle-men you see working in the fields. He was really strong and kind of rough-looking. I acted as though I had to go into the kitchen for the milk pot. I called out to my friend. His name's Budjee. He comes to the kitchen door and smiles. I made signs and he whispered. 'He's my' — and he puts his hand down on his hard penis — 'guru'. Shiva I tell you if you want action, then make it three guys."

Shiva lay in silence. He wanted to ask Ramu more but all Ramu would say was "Good night."

The cricket match went on all day. It was a serious challenge match, but it also had a picnic air about it. Each player had put in ten rupees for lunch and drinks. The Studs had arranged for the Deeva Hotel at the railway gate to supply packed lunches. Abdullah's mother came and cut up limes and mixed thirty litres of squash in two large red plastic drums. In the afternoon break Sreenu's father sent cold Thumbs-Up and Limca drinks with their servants. The Studs won the toss and batted. After lunch they all sat around under the peepal trees on the north side of the ground.

Abdullah said so that everyone could hear, "How about shifting me up in the batting order, just one place. If I'm batting near sunset you know what will happen."

Everyone made a rather embarrassed laugh. A few months before in the inter-school social match Abdullah's father had stormed onto the pitch and shouted at Abdullah for not being home and getting ready for prayers. In the middle of batting he had to leave. His father was really weird. He would allow his wife and daughters to come and make lime squash for the match. He gave a really good shirt piece for the 'man of the match' — but he was strict on times for prayer.

Reddy the captain said, "You change with Shiva or Naidu according to the time, okay." Abdullah finished up changing with Naidu and got run out for two. At the close the Studs lost by ten runs and two wickets. The "man of the match" went without question to Shiva. He took two wickets with his spin bowling, took a catch at silly point, and astounded himself with two four's and a total of 32 runs. Ramu had willingly accepted being number two umpire and scorer.

They walked home in high spirits. Shanti was sitting on the front verandah with three other young women. Shiva put his foot on the bottom step as the temple bell started. Shanti looked at him and said, "I'd be over there quickly if I was you, comments have already been made."

Ramu looked at Shiva. They ran inside and washed quickly, put on white lunghis and ran out of the house to the temple.

An hour and a half later when they came out of the temple and crossed the road, Shiva saw Sam sitting on the verandah talking to Shanti and playing with the children. Shiva sat down on the step.

To Shiva, Sam was his closest friend. They shared many secrets. Sam was strictly a 'womanizer' as he put it. He almost disapproved of Shiva for masturbating so much. When Shiva had told him about what had happened two years ago Sam was amazed. Sam's constant goal was to save up 'for one'. He would skip a tea, miss a film, walk to save a bus fare, just to 'make a visit'. Sam had thought it a great joke of Shiva's about it being very convenient that the brothel line was just behind the Government Hospital.

Sam was sitting on the verandah, he had never been inside their house. He never made a move and Shiva never invited him. They both knew the situation and felt silence on the subject was best. Sam's family was 'scheduled caste', bottom rung of the ladder. If that wasn't enough they were also Christians. Shiva knew it must have really been a thorn for his father to have to ask favours and pay money to get Shiva into St. Thomas's English-medium Arts and Science College.

Shanti must have seen her father coming. She went inside. Sam, Shiva and Ramu sat on the verandah edge talking. Shiva's father ignored them as he walked up the steps. Sam was full of stories about the bookshop. Ramu was extolling Shiva's cricket ability. They chatted on and on. When Shiva told Sam that he was going to visit his aunt Sam smiled but said nothing.

Sam encouraged Ramu to do well in the interview because he thought that a job with the Corot company was really good and well paid. "If you get a clerical job and get onto shift work they pay really well," Sam explained in detail.

A bell rang inside the house — mother's signal. Sam nodded and they said their goodbyes.

"Tell you all about it when I come back, Sam," Shiva said.

Sam grinned as he walked off: "No thanks," and they laughed and waved to each other.

After supper Shiva's mother called him into the kitchen. "Now go to bed early and no talking all night to Ramu. I'll wake you at five and have things ready for you. In this basket are all the food preparations for aunt. In this carrier there are pickles so make sure you keep it upright or it might leak oil. In this bag I've put spices and tamarind. On the top tomorrow morning I'll put your food for the train and the water bottle." She paused. "Now is there anything else?" She looked around, "No, and here's the money. That should be enough, be careful on the train with everything. Count the bags and make sure you keep the money safely inside your pants pocket. Not in your shirt. That's how your brother-in-law lost his money remember." She looked around again. "Anything else?"

Shiva looked at the basket, the container and the bag. He would also have his own shoulder-bag with clothing. "No, I really only need an elephant or six porters to carry it all." His mother wasn't amused.

He and Ramu walked down to his room, but it was quite some time before they fell asleep.

"If you had a chance, who would you invite to join us from your cricket team to make three in this?"

They were sitting close together, facing each other, legs crossed over each other, naked and excited and exciting each other.

Shiva didn't answer. He didn't think anyone would...

"I don't mean who you think would, but who would you like?"

Shiva smiled. "If it was like so, well, if I could just make it happen you mean, well," he paused, "Laxman. I think he is really, well, nice. I mean body nice, as well as being a nice guy."

They sat silently together for a few minutes, just running their hands over each other. Ramu slowly lay Shiva down, while he remained sitting. He leaned forward over Shiva, who knew what he was going to do. Shiva closed his eyes, then he moved suddenly and sat up and pushed Ramu's head away. It was starting to happen too quickly. Ramu leaned towards him and blew softly in his ear. Shiva felt his body tingle. Ramu took both hands and gently brushed Shiva's face, then came close and kissed him. At first the kiss was just on the lips and then it went deeper. It was strange and confusing. Shiva wrapped his arms around Ramu and they kissed again.

Shiva now gently lay Ramu down, leaned forward and brushed his lips over his pubic hair. He drew Ramu into his mouth and Ramu's hips moved slowly up and down. Shiva kept moving his mouth on and over, drawing Ramu deeper into him. He ran one hand under Ramu's testicles and squeezed them gently. Ramu was almost pulsating; Shiva saw his legs go stiff. He drew back and ran both hands up and down Ramu's stomach and chest slowly. He ran his fingers through his hair. It was a new and deep sensational feeling for Shiva. He realised that what he was doing to Ramu was the fulfillment of many dreams and ideas and fantasies of the last two years.

Ramu sat up. "I agree, Laxman is really good-looking isn't he? But I will tell you who I think would join us in a three-way deal." He looked quizzically at Shiva, who was wondering who he thought would be interested in this type of game.

"One guy this afternoon was really looking around and a few times I caught him looking at other guys' 'places'."

Shiva whispered, "You sure it wasn't me? I'm always looking at guys' places to see what bulges are there."

They smiled at each other.

"I'll tell you — ready?" Ramu asked, and Shiva nodded. "Abdullah".

Shiva looked wide-eyed. "Abdullah!"

"Yes, and I'm not joking, he was looking at you twice."

"Really, Ramu, I think that he is the most hunky-looking guy. He has such long long legs. I love to watch him bowl. I saw him once with his shirt off early this summer when we were practising. He is into weights you know. I just never thought he would be interested in even looking at guys. I thought," Shiva paused, "I suppose it's stupid isn't it? I thought that being a Muslim he wouldn't be interested."

Ramu was rubbing his fingers across Shiva's back near his hips and the feeling was making Shiva even more excited. Ramu's other hand was under Shiva's balls with one finger pressed tightly against Shiva's scrotum. Ramu ran his hand around and across Shiva's belly and then down and over his hard head. "Hey, look, see that, some fluid has already leaked out, they call that 'pre-cum' or something like that. You are really excited aren't you?"

Shiva blinked. "I'm about to explode with excitement." He was holding Ramu tightly and then couldn't resist the urge to snuggle down between Ramu's arms and put his mouth deep over Ramu who soon groaned and pulled away.

"I bet Abdullah is in bed now masturbating himself and thinking about you and me and wondering, maybe even thinking that we wouldn't dare do anything like this because we are Brahmins. It's got nothing to do with what our religion is or what our families are. We are what we are."

Shiva had often wondered what he was. What these feelings really meant. He knew that he wasn't like those men he saw dressed, kind of like women, selling vegetables in the market. "What are we Ramu?"

Ramu leaned close, and then kissed him gently. "We are simply men who love men."

For months afterwards Ramu's words would ring in Shiva's mind. They exactly described how he felt. He was a man and he loved other men.

They lay down and faced each other. They held each other and came within seconds of each other. Coming together like that really made a deeper feeling in Shiva. They fell asleep.

Shiva woke up before his mother or anyone called him. He went into the courtyard and took a bath with cold water. It woke him up nicely. When he was dressed he found a pen and paper, and wrote:

> Dear Ramuji guru,
>   Thanks for everything and all. I hope you do well in the interview. Really hope you get the job and come and stay with us — me. Take this shirt material that I won yesterday as a gift from one man to another man. Please write to me in ten days. I'll be home by then. I'll write you too.
>   Love, Shivaji

He folded the note, put it on the shirt cloth and then put Ramu's toothpaste tube on top of that. He couldn't miss it then. Shiva picked up his bag and walked down to the prayer room. He lit the Nataraj oil lamp and this time he did say a prayer. For himself and the trip, for Ramu and his interview. He said a 'thank you' in his mind for having the chances he was getting, including the chance to love, even if it was with a man.

He took incense sticks and lit them. He placed some on the Nataraj idol base and the others he wedged into the frame of Krishna. His father walked by, stopped and waited for him. As he came out his father took his hand and raised it to the bell and they rang it together. Shiva didn't know whether his father held his hand to do it in case he thought he would forget, or because he was somehow being friendly or fatherly. Shiva never knew what his father really thought or felt about him.

Two Years Ago...

IT WAS two years ago that very month that he made his first visit to his aunt's. He called it his first visit because he had come by himself. As a child he had often come with the others. Two years ago he had come by himself and it had been his first big train trip alone. He had enjoyed it immensely. There was a kind of freedom being alone on the train without his family. Without his father. Without his older brother. Before he took the train two years ago his father had made him sit for two hours writing and repeating instructions. Shiva supposed some people might have thought it caring that his father spent such time giving travelling instructions. Shiva knew that it was just his way of enforcing his will on their lives, but he had always been fascinated by the urchins who seemed even younger than him. They travelled without tickets, without anyone, and made money out of it.

At Chintana he had been put on the train by his father and elder brother. His father had checked the bogey number, the seat number and the passenger list three times to make sure he was in the correct place. He then asked people sitting near Shiva to "Look after him". This made Shiva embarrassed. The train pulled out on time, everyone waved. Two minutes later two of the men were asleep and the others were playing cards. He walked up and down the carriage and no one took any notice of him.

When the train stopped at his station he did as his father instructed, knowing full well that Aunt would report on him after his stay with her.

He alighted and stood on the platform for a minute, looked around and saw the Station Master's Office and headed for it. He hadn't got halfway when he felt a tap on the shoulder. It was Aunt smiling down at him.

"So you have arrived. I watched you get down. Very good. You are careful with your bags I see. Three in all. Let me guess what's in them." She didn't though, just turned and spoke to the young man next to her, "Chinni, take young Shiva's bags and arrange the rickshaw please. Let's not stay here longer than needed. It's not clean air."

Chinni left quickly and Aunt started to follow. "Have your journey ticket ready Shivaji for the ticket collector."

They passed through the gate, Aunt first handing over her platform ticket with a nod. He walked beside her. "In one of the bags I have my study books. I got some old ones that are for next year's subjects. I want to read them in advance."

She nodded and kept walking.

Chinni was waiting with a rickshaw. He had his bicycle and on the back were tied Shiva's bags.

On the way home Aunt hardly spoke. She sat with a handkerchief over her mouth and nose. She took up most of the rickshaw seat, wedging Shiva, thin as he was, into the corner, against the side bar that dug into his ribs. She kept pulling her sari tighter and tighter over her head. As they got to the corner where she lived she said, "Ohh dear I do hate going to that smelly railway station. And what's more these roads are so dusty nowadays. Those lorries make so much sound with their horns." She paused. "The dust gives me nose problems you know?"

He didn't think it was a question. He nodded though and half smiled. Shiva had been fascinated watching Chinni. He weaved in and out of the traffic keeping abreast with the rickshaw like a circus performer. He made it look artful. He could brake quickly and start again without putting his feet down for balance. Shiva watched him most of the way. He turned and smiled to Shiva a few times. He was a hairy young guy but his moustache was thin. When he pushed down on the pedals Shiva saw his muscles bulge.

The whole day Aunt made a fuss of him. He slept most of the afternoon, having eaten far too much at lunchtime. He had no option with Aunt. She had said a hundred times that he was far to thin. She was determined to fatten him, send him home like a prize peacock. He had to admit though that her coconut sweet was rather good.

In the evening she went off to the temple telling him to watch the house and tell Chinni the servant boy if he needed anything. He had been sent to stay with her because over the next ten days she was going to special pujas at the temple, followed by discourses. A well-known swami had come from Calcutta.

He didn't know what he was supposed to guard. She wore all her gold to the temple. The radio was an old model. The furniture didn't look special, and then there were only pots and things in the kitchen. Besides what was Chinni going to do? What she did the rest of the year for a guard he didn't know. He didn't really care because it was a holiday from home. He had books to study too. His father wasn't there either — that was great. Two weeks without his father constantly questioning him. Two weeks without his brother treating him like a peon. He walked around the house. He grinned when he saw the locks on the doors. They were the same big type they had on the temple at his place. The keys were as thick as his little fingers. The windows not only had bolts but also wooden bars. He shrugged and sat next to the radio and tried to find some music. There was music but it was the kind he hated.

It was to be two weeks in which he could study quietly. He had slipped from fifth place to eighth. His father had blamed his spending so much time at cricket practice. His marks weren't bad but his father said they were. Shiva thought that eighth out of sixty-five in the class wasn't too bad really. But he would aim at getting back in the top five. He didn't want to have his cricket stopped.

He heard Aunt coming up the steps. She smiled, went into the kitchen, and served supper for both of them. She sat facing him, adding extra curry as soon as he finished one spoonful. She told him about the visiting swami and how very wise and interesting he was. He was actually surprised she hadn't dragged him to the temple.

He thought that all the swamis he had ever heard all went on about the same impossible thing. They all extolled being so good that there would be no reincarnation after death. How it was possible for humans to be so perfect Shiva couldn't imagine. He did not express his views to his aunt. The swamis all looked alike and they all seemed to sing out of tune. They all expected everyone to abstain from almost everything that Shiva though was pleasant! Still they were always fat and well cared for. He didn't think that they really worked. Going from one place to the other, sitting comfortably on cushions telling the same jargon to people. He didn't think that his father really worked either. Being a pujari, a priest who simply performed rituals, wasn't what Shiva called a 'real job'.

After supper he went upstairs and sat on the balcony for a while, then went to bed and quickly fell asleep.

He was woken up by Chinni standing next to his bed. "Hot water in the bathroom. Aunt says to have bath quickly and come down for breakfast it's ready."

Shiva waited for Chinni to leave before getting out of bed. He wondered if Chinni had seen his erection under the bed sheet. He'd been lying on his back when Chinni woke him. It was still stiff when he took his shorts off and pissed, after closing the bathroom door. There was no lock on the door, but it stuck at the bottom against the frame.

When he went downstairs he had to eat three of the largest iddlis he had ever seen, covered with ghee and served with a plate of coconut chutney. He heard Aunt talking to Chinni about going to the market.

"May I go to the market with Chinni too?"

She turned and looked at him with some surprise. "What do you want there? He can get it for you. The sun is already hot. It's very dusty and smelly there too. I can't imagine anyone wanting to go when it can be fetched for you."

She handed money to Chinni. "Better you get on with your

studies. Bring your books down to the front room. It's very good reading light there, and a breeze will come in that window first. It's a quiet room too."

At five in the evening Aunt announced that she was leaving early. "To tell the truth I've been invited to have tiffin with a friend of mine, then we will go to bhajans together. You brush your hair. The walk with me to her place will be good for you."

He presumed that it wasn't near to the smelly market. The sky was still bright and cloudless — a soft clear blue. The sun was well angled but the pink had not started to creep across the horizon. They stopped at one corner and Aunt bartered with the woman for a string of jasmine and a handful of marigold flowers that the woman wrapped in a leaf. They turned down the wide side street. It was lined on both sides with huge overhanging old banyan trees. It was very cool. The houses all had high compound walls. They were the big old types set back from the road.

On some of the gates were marble plaques with the house name engraved. Many had signs: BEWARE OF THE DOG. He smiled and thought they could have a sign on their front door at home: BEWARE OF THE FATHER.

"What are you smiling at Shivaji?" Aunt had caught his smile.

"Ohhh, a big dog sign and a small dog."

She stopped at a gate. It was wrought iron and had a brass handle. In the driveway was a white Ambassador car. A young man was in the driveway playing with a small dog. There was no dog sign on the gate. The dog ran up to the gate and wagged its tail. It looked very well cared for. A red collar was around its neck. Aunt spoke to the dog. The young man came up the drive. He was tall and thin, Shiva thought he was really beautiful. His skin was a soft bronze brown colour. He had shorts on, and Shiva noticed the fine hair on his legs. He had a thin moustache that might have been trimmed at the ends, it was so neat.

The young man smiled. "Hello Aunty, mother is expecting you, she is waiting inside. Let me hold the dog and open the gate for you."

He seemed very friendly and called her Aunt. They must be good friends, Shiva thought. Aunt didn't allow too many non-family people to be that friendly. The boy looked too bronzed to be a Brahmin though.

Aunt turned to Shiva. He thought she was about to introduce hm. He was wrong. "Thank you Shiva, you can go back now, don't dawdle either. There is no one in the house you know."

Somehow it sounded as though Chinni wasn't a proper person or something. He stood for a second and smiled at her. He turned slightly to smile at the young man, but he was bending over patting the dog. Shiva turned quickly and briskly walked down the road towards Aunt's house. If she was watching, and he knew she would be, he might get marks for that! Maybe...

He rang the door bell and heard Chinni come and lift the wooden bar. He smiled and Chinni smiled back. He crossed the room and heard the wood drop back on the catch. He walked up to his room and lay on the bed, thinking about the young man he had seen, and the dog.

He wasn't sure how long he had been there dreaming. A soft knock startled him. Shiva knew that it must be Chinni. He looked at the small bedside clock Aunt had put on the bedside table. It couldn't be tiffin time. The door opened slowly. Chinni put his head in.

"You went out walking, would you like some hot water to bathe before having tiffin? There is a pot ready in the kitchen if you want me to bring it up for you."

Chinni spoke without expression on his face. Shiva realised he was almost staring at him though. He thought that Chinni looked a bit like the young man he had been thinking about. Only older, more mature. And, yes, somehow less innocent looking. More physically mature.

Of course he was much less innocent, Shiva thought. He most likely had a dozen experiences with girls around the town. Shiva sat up. "Yes, alright, bring the hot water. I think I will have a bath before tiffin and starting to study again."

Shiva heard Chinni go down the stairs two at a time, a light thud thud thud. He took off his shirt and pants, put on a cotton towel and picked up his soap and walked to the bathroom. He still had his shorts on under the towel. There were already two buckets in the bathroom, one empty and the other filled with cold water. He put his towel on the wooden peg. He stretched up and looked through the high small window. He could only see sky, and it was almost dark.

The pink he had seen walking home was now turning to grey. He liked the greys of the evening that slipped across the sky just as the stars started to shine. He stood staring out of the window and wondered where the moon would be. He then realised it would be on the other side of the house. He hardly heard the door open. He turned to see Chinni put the pot of hot water on the floor. He poured some of the cold water into the empty bucket and started to mix hot water. He dipped his little finger into it.

"You can make it hotter if you want. There is plenty of hot water in the pot."

Shiva bent over and tested the water. It was alright, he didn't want it too hot. He noticed that while Chinni was downstairs he had taken his shirt off. He didn't like to stare too much. He could easily see the long line of hair that ran from his throat down to his navel and disappeared somewhere into the lunghi. Two small fans of hair spread across his chest. He was muscular and very wiry, the kind of person Shiva thought who could work hard and not feel the strain. He didn't know for sure, that was just his idea.

Chinni went to the bathroom door. "There is no one in the house, you can take your shorts off to bathe if you wish. Put them in the bucket and I'll rinse them later and put them on the line to dry for you."

He smiled and closed the door, but not hard against the frame. What a strange thing to say Shiva thought. He often bathed without his shorts in his bathroom at home. He knew that many of his friends never took them off to bathe. They would bathe, dry and then wrapping the towel around themselves, stand wriggling and pulling the shorts off. He had seen many boys do it and the wriggling always made him laugh to himself. They looked like they were doing some crazy dance. It had been the topic of a lunchtime discussion between Sam, Sreenu, Ramana, Laxman and Abdullah. Like many of their conversations at school it started and ended nowhere.

Shiva knelt beside the bucket and poured one mug of warm water over himself slowly, then another. He was thinking of the young guy with the dog and it was making his penis hard. He squeezed it for a few seconds, felt that unique sensation, and tucked it between his legs. Then all he could see was the little bunch of thick black hair. He picked up the soap, ran it over his head and worked his fingers around to make a thick lather. He closed his eyes tight and put the soap down so that even with his eyes closed he could find it. He poured water over his head and started to make soap lather again. He thought he heard the door, but he couldn't open his eyes. Then a little light swept across his face and he knew that the door must have opened.

Chinni spoke. "You want me to pour water over you?"

Shiva wasn't sure if he wanted Chinni to pour water or not. He didn't have much option as he heard the mug being lifted from the bucket and felt the warm water running nicely over his back. Chinni then massaged his scalp with soap, poured a little more water and made it lather again. He paused. Then Shiva, with his eyes still closed tightly against the soapy water, felt Chinni rubbing soap across his shoulders, across and down his back. Shiva was glad he had tucked his hard penis between his legs. He would be embarrassed if Chinni saw it.

Chinni rubbed his back gently, then moved down to his thighs. A exciting feeling crept through Shiva. He felt his tucked-away penis go even harder. With a strange shock he realised that Chinni was now rubbing soap over his buttocks. Suddenly a new exciting feeling gripped Shiva. Chinni was rubbing his soaped hand all over his testicles and up and down his hard penis. He stayed kneeling, not really knowing what to do. Chinni took his hand away and poured water all over Shiva. Shiva wiped his face and looked up. Chinni didn't have his lunghi on, just his shorts, where there was something poking hard against the material. Shiva looked up at Chinni and saw that he was smiling. Not grinning, just smiling. It was a soft kind smile, a knowing smile. Shiva felt that his whole body was alive in a new way.

"With all this extra hot water I could also take a bath." Chinni paused. "If you don't mind?"

For a few seconds Shiva was confused. It always happened when someone was friendly and then used that 'master-servant' tone. The tone of 'upper and lower caste' used just as often by those who were so disgustingly called lower caste. Shiva always had to control himself when this happened. Chinni had just washed his hair and rubbed his back and run his hand over his balls and hard cock. Now he was asking if he could bathe next to him! Shiva knew it was his caste that perpetuated this injustice. Why in a so-called free India did people still accept it?

He smiled and shrugged his shoulders. It was the same shrug that many of the guys made at school when caste things came up. In their group it didn't happen much. Sometimes though a new guy would be with them. The shrug was meant to show a non-recognition of anything that smacked of some taboo that was outdated, unwanted and demeaning. But Shiva knew that deep inside very many of them this rubbish still permeated their lives. Usually it was somehow imposed by elders and parents.

Shiva played cricket with a friend, a so called 'harijan' lower-caste boy. His name was Ram. A brilliant guy to know if you needed a quick answer in physics. Ram always seemed embarrassed to offer or take anything from other students who he thought were 'upper'. Sometimes even a glass of water seemed a problem. And of course there were still 'backward' Brahmin students who thought it was right or smart to pull their caste rank. All of Shiva's close friends made stinging remarks when others showed this leftover shit.

The worst was 'Brahmin' Murty Ramana. One day when he made a show over water, not once but twice, the three of them held him down. Each pissed on his legs. They put spit on their fingers and ran it across his forehead. He couldn't believe what was happening. He said nothing. Next day he came to school smiling and told them just before the bell rang, "I didn't bathe last night or this morning, so if I smell of piss it's your bad luck."

What Shiva was really wondering was if Chinni would take his shorts off too. With a smile and a quick movement Chinni did just that. He flung the shorts over to the wooden hook on the wall. Shiva turned just slightly to see if they caught on the hook. In turning his own hard cock flipped up from being tucked tight between his legs. It thumped on his stomach. They were both looking at each other — more precisely, at each other's cocks. Chinni came and knelt in the same position in front of Shiva. He took hold of his cock and was slowly drawing the foreskin back and forth.

"Is this what you do?" he asked with a smile.

Shiva shook his head. "No. All I do is hold it like this," he took his own now very hard cock and held it near the head, "and I just squeeze it like this. It makes so much feeling that I have to stop after a few minutes."

Chinni leaned across and taking Shiva's hand away put his own there and started to work the foreskin up and down. "Does thick white stuff come out when you just squeeze it?"

Shiva sat still thinking. "No."

He realised then that he knew what Chinni was talking about. It was the semen stuff that came out inside a woman when you had sex and mixed with the woman's stuff and made babies. He knew that much from Pradeep's biology book. He was not into botany and biology — pulling flowers apart and cutting up frogs and rats and stuff. His interest was chemistry and physics and maths. He had read it in Pradeep's book when they were asking each other revision questions for some term exam.

Chinni took Shiva's hand and placed it around his own cock.

Shiva was filled with so many different new feelings he didn't speak. He mouth felt dry. He was holding Chinni's cock and doing the same to him, running the foreskin up and down. Something was happening to Shiva. His body was filled with strange and exciting sensations. He enjoyed holding Chinni's penis like this. He had often thought about doing this and other things with his friends, but there had never been a chance. He had often wondered what it would be like. Now he was experiencing it, he was holding someone else's. It was hard and much bigger than his, and it felt good. He was fascinated to feel something so thick and long. He imagined that one day his would also grow big.

Then his mind went blank. He felt this... sensation grip him. He thought at first it was pain. Then he thought he was going to piss. But it wasn't pain and no piss came — it was so different and it somehow numbed him. He was going to tell Chinni to stop, but he couldn't.

Then he felt something happening, something deep inside his crotch, somewhere inside his balls. A strangely new exciting searing sensation ran up his cock. His legs went stiff. A fluid shot out, not once but three times. He instantly knew what it was. This was Pradeep's book in reality. He felt his body unwind as though he had been wound up like a clock spring. He knew this must be semen. He felt excited and relaxed and exhilarated. He looked at the semen. The first two shots had landed on Chinni's arm and the last one on his hairy leg.

He was still holding Chinni's cock and pulling the skin up and down. All of a sudden Chinni groaned and started to bend towards Shiva. He stopped, he thought Chinni must be in pain. As soon as Shiva let go, Chinni grabbed it and moved the skin up and down fast. Shiva watched fascinated now. Then the semen shot out thick and milky. It landed on Shiva's stomach and leg.

Chinni smiled and relaxed and leaned back on his legs. Shiva was still squatting too, just holding his still hard penis and moving the skin up and down very slowly. Fascinated with himself, almost.

They just sat looking at each other peacefully.

Shiva was thinking. He had learnt the word for this in English. The word for doing this, with your hand, not inside a woman. It was called masturbation. Pradeep had showed him the word, Shiva had read it and not commented because it had confused him. The explanation had said 'self abuse'. Shiva had thought that this meant to hurt oneself sexually. What they had just done together was to masturbate. He couldn't see how it was an abuse.

It wasn't painful. It was, he thought, the opposite. He didn't really know what word to use in his mind for the feelings that had engulfed him. He smiled. 'Fantastic' would do for now.

His first question to Chinni was, "How many times can you do this, I mean, every day, or what?"

Chinni thought, or looked thoughtful. He was pouring water over Shiva's stomach and legs. "Some men say that if you do it too many times you will get weak. Lose your energy. I've been doing it every day since I was fifteen and now I'm twenty. So that's a full five years. I work just as hard as any man. I don't think I'm weak."

He paused and smiled. "I watched a rooster once. He would chase hens around every morning and afternoon when I let him out. He screws every hen he can catch, struts around like a peacock afterwards. He forgets he is just a rooster. I reckon I'm as good as any of those cocks." Chinni laughed and Shiva laughed with him. "I'd sooner get a tired arm from doing this than pulling water from your aunt's well in the summer." He stood up and taking Shiva's arm pulled him up too. They stood drying each other.

Chinni collected their shorts, the empty pot and bucket and went downstairs. Shiva smiled when he heard him going down the steps two at a time. He walked to his room. He didn't want to study! He did wish though that he had Pradeep's textbook with him. He just lay on the bed thinking about how great it had felt.

He felt somehow that he was free of something. It wasn't definable, but it was there. He felt almost released from something. He felt that some secret that had been locked up in him was now out and free, open.

He heard the front-door bolts being opened. It must be near nine o'clock and Aunt was returning. He got up quickly and put his shirt on, buttoning it up as he went down the stairs. He was hungry. That would make Aunt happy.

After supper Aunt went quickly around locking doors and sent him to his room. A silence fell over the inner house. He lay on his bed. His penis was hard again. He wondered if Chinni would masturbate tomorrow, and if he would do it with him. He had liked the feeling of holding Chinni's hard cock. He wanted to hold it again. He wanted to run his hands over his hairy chest. He wanted to feel his muscular arms.

He fell asleep with a new sense of contentment.

However on the next afternoon he saw his fantasy for the planned evening dissolve.

"This evening you will have to be in the house by yourself Shiva, Chinni babu is coming with me. I have all of these rice cakes to take to the temple and distribute to the poor at the gate. He won't return until I come home. You will have to be careful."

She stood up and rubbed her back. "If you are going to bathe this evening, do it early if you want hot water. I want to lock the kitchen outer door."

Chinni was sitting and packing the rice cakes into a basket. "If it's too early for you to bathe before we leave, I'll heat up some water for you when we return."

Aunt clicked her tongue. "What nonsense fellow. Talking about bathing at nine o'clock in the night. Really you are senseless at times. Anyway," she paused, "it's a waste of firewood."

Chinni kept his head down and went on packing the cakes. Shiva caught his eye a few seconds later and they communicated that their dream had been shattered.

Shiva knew that Chinni slept in the outer verandah room and Aunt would lock that side when she went to bed. He waited for them to leave. He knew that he had plenty of studying to do. He knew too that his mind wouldn't be on his work. It was like trying to study three hours before going to see a new movie, or the next night after seeing a super movie. He sat in the front room and listened to the radio for a while. He got bored. It was the type of classical music his father liked. He turned it off. He thought that it sounded like people in pain.

All day he had been feeling the urge to do it again. He would wait until everyone had gone to bed that evening. He went upstairs and decided to bathe while the water was warm. He had an erection the whole time he was bathing. In the end he couldn't wait. He knelt in the same place and position as he and Chinni Babu had been the day before. He masturbated himself slowly remembering yesterday.

The only part missing was Chinni, Chinni holding his cock, and him holding Chinni's. That was the bit he desired!

The time passed slowly. At 9.15 he took a study book down and sat in the front room.

He heard Aunt and Chinni coming up the steps. He jumped up and unlocked and opened the door. "Now look Shiva I have a terrible headache. I sat too near to that loud P.A. system. My head is unbearable. Chinni babu will get your supper. You will have to manage yourself. I'm going to bed." She handed Shiva the keys, "Lock up carefully and double-check the locks." She turned to Chinni: "And you, don't make a mess serving the food. The kitchen's clean you know."Aunt held her head and walked towards her bedroom. They heard the door close and then the bolt lock.

They looked at each other with a knowing sly smile. Chinni winked at Shiva, and Shiva felt himself blush. A wink was what a hero gave a heroine in a Hindu movie. A wink was something secret, somehow connected with love and sex. They went into the kitchen and ate together — something that would have horrified Aunt if she knew. Chinni took the plates outside to the cleaning square, came in, smiled and closed the door quietly putting the keys on the right hook.

They went upstairs together silently, holding hands. Chinni turned and closed the door at the top of the stairs and dropped the wooden bar. He turned and put his arms around Shiva and smiled and hugged him.

Shiva smiled back and said, "I couldn't wait." He paused. "I mean, I've already..." He paused again, he didn't really know how to say what he had done, this new discovery! "I thought that it wouldn't be possible together tonight."

Chinni just grinned. "I thought you might have done; neither of us could have thought that poor Aunt would have a headache." He smiled and added, "Want to try again?"

Shiva didn't know if it would come out again so soon, the semen, but he knew something. His penis was starting to get hard again just thinking and talking about it. He also knew that if it didn't happen for him, he could do it for Chinni, to Chinni. The thought of that, holding Chinni's cock and watching Chinni, made him really hard.

They were standing on the open roof verandah. Chinni leaned across the distance between them and drew his hand up between Shiva's legs. The sensation made Shiva shudder with excitement. He drew the hand slowly across his crotch and pressed slightly on the already hard cock, and Shiva felt it twitch.

Shiva couldn't resist the urge, the temptation to do the same to Chinni and with daring pulled his lunghi up quickly. He slid his other hand under the lunghi and rubbed Chinni's hard cock still imprisoned inside the shorts. He stepped even closer and slid one hand up the leg of the shorts and rubbed the end of the cock. There was already some fluid there.

Chinni hugged him close. They moved into the bedroom. Standing together they took each other's clothing off slowly. Shiva couldn't manage the pin that held Chinni's shorts up. Chinni flicked it open with a smile. The shorts fell down and stopped when they hung on his cock. Shiva slipped his hand inside the shorts and flicked the cock out. It was like a spring. They stood there for a long time, Chinni just letting Shiva explore him. Shiva ran his hands all over Chinni's body, up and down his chest and stomach. From the balls, which he caressed, around the pubic 'nest' and up through the hair that ran in a fine line to Chinni's throat. Shiva felt exhilarated being able to feel the hair on Chinni's stomach and chest. Looking into Chinni's eyes and watching the expression on his face, Shiva knew that he was enjoying it too!

Chinni moved to the bed and they sat facing each other, legs intertwined. Then Chinni did something that blanked Shiva's mind out. He leaned over and took Shiva's penis in his mouth. It was just so contrary to everything a Brahmin learnt. With all of the taboos about this hand for that and this hand for other things, saliva not meant to be swallowed, fingers not touching the mouth when eating. Now Chinni had his cock in his mouth. Shiva's mind stopped. For the first few seconds, the first few movements, he was shocked. He felt himself go tense with a shock of disgust. He was going to pull Chinni's head away. But between thinking of the protest and the words to express it the realization struck, the realization of having a hard erect cock being sucked for the first time.

In an instant, the sensation of what was happening overran all the old taboos! The feeling was indescribable, he had never imagined such a sensation could exist!

Chinni withdrew his mouth and raised his head to look at Shiva. Shiva just sat motionless with excitement. He blinked his eyes a few times and sighed a little. This was an unbelievable sensation. He, Shiva, knew now exactly what he wanted to do.

The day before he was due to go home Shiva felt a sudden fit of depression. He knew what he was going home to. How could he live without this, this everything? How would he ever find a friend like Chinni again? A new and exciting page had opened. A short chapter, and Shiva saw it closing.

"You must be homesick Shiva, you don't look happy." Aunt put her hand on his shoulder. "Still it's only until tomorrow and you will be home. Cheer up."

He smiled pleasantly at Aunt.

On the train home he slept the whole way. He was so tired. He and Chinni had hardly slept two hours that last night together. The elderly man on the berth below him woke him just as the train crossed the river, about fifteen minutes from Chintana. He got up and taking his small toilet bag walked slowly to the bathroom at the end of the bogey. He waited his turn, bending down and looking out at the rice fields as the train slowed at the junction lines. He began to feel depressed. Somehow he wished the train would just keep on going, and not stop. That he and it could just travel on.

The thought of being home and his father's demanding ways, his brother's jibes, his brother-in-law's snide comments made him feel listless.

A few minutes after he had returned from the bathroom and sat down the train began to slow again. He picked up his luggage and walked to the door. The train had slowed down at the crossing signal. When it eventually chugged and stopped at the platform he almost let the crowd just push him along the platform. He looked around disinterestedly to see if anyone was there to meet him. He was glad he saw no one. Shiva thought about walking home, but then he knew his father would want to know why he took so long to reach home after the train had arrived. Whatever excuse he used for walking home instead of taking a rickshaw would be criticised or commented on. He managed to get through the day smiling and not showing his real feelings, telling everyone about his stay with Aunt. Well not quite all — just the edited and censored version. In the evening he stood in front of the mirror. He looked at himself. There weren't any signs of change, but changed he had...

Back in the Present...

HIS MOTHER had breakfast ready for him. She was well organised. A rickshaw was waiting outside.

The train arrived on time and as it slowed down Shiva ran beside a carriage and dropped his handkerchief on a seat to make that time-honoured Indian train reservation. The train was crowded. The passengers surged out in a wave, then he was carried on with the in-going crowd. It was a struggle with the basket, carrier and two bags. He reached his handkerchief-reserved seat and looked up to see the top berth still vacant. He quickly put his basket and bags along it. He sat on the seat until the train pulled out and then asked the man next to him to keep his space as he was going up on the upper berth to sleep. He also asked him to wake him at Badrapur station. The middle-aged man nodded, and gave him his case to keep in the corner of the upper berth too. Shiva needed the sleep. He smiled to himself. Not tired like every student from late studies, but tired from having another man to love. He felt extremely happy...

The man woke him about five minutes before Badrapur and he climbed down. He took his toilet bag and went to the bathroom and washed his hands and face. It helped to wake him up — so did the smell in the train toilet! When he got back he found the man now had a window seat opposite him and was reading the latest *Sports Review.* Imran Khan the cricketer was on the cover.

The train pulled into the station with a couple of jerky chugs that made passengers standing in the aisles grab the seats nearest to them. He took the parcel down with his tiffin meal in it and was about to start eating when the man stood up and put the magazine on his seat and walked out to the platform. Shiva put his tiffin to one side and leant over and picked it up. He had no sooner opened it when a passenger thinking the seat was empty nearly sat down before Shiva 'saved' it. He placed his tiffin there instead and went on reading, or looking at the pictures first. The man came back and Shiva quickly retrieved his tiffin and smiling put the sports magazine back.

The man offered Shiva a banana. "You can read the magazine if you wish. In fact you can keep it. I buy it regularly but never take it home, my wife scolds me for wasting money if she sees it."

The young man at the end of the seat leaned forward and laughed. "My wife smells my breath every time I come home from the office and raises merry if she smells tobacco."

They all laughed, except a woman on the side seat who scowled at them all.

Shiva took the magazine and thanked the man and slipped it in his shoulder-bag. He would keep it to read at Aunt's, and to show Chinni babu. He was sure he would like to see the full middle-page poster of the Australian hockey team that was coming to India next month.

Looking out of the window he saw the large green mosque dome and knew it would only be about five minutes to the station. Some of the passengers were already moving towards the door. He waited until he saw the big Shiva Temple come into view. He sat very still and watched carefully. Yes, he saw the roof of his aunt's house for just a second. He thought he saw a sari blowing in the breeze from the roof but he wasn't sure.

He waited until the first rush of passengers surged out and got on the end of the crowd. He was really loaded up. By the time he reached the door a few passengers were already pushing on. He shouted rudely at a fat man with a large bedroll trying to struggle through. The man looked quite shocked to be shouted at. Shiva didn't care and as the man pushed by he gave him a short kick that must have hurt.

He stood on the platform for a minute to catch his breath and adjust his things. Two porters must have thought he was unable to manage and started to browbeat him into carrying the bags. He impolitely told them he didn't need them. He looked around, not really expecting to see anyone. He walked out and after a short argument with a young muscular-looking, dark and hairy rickshaw wallah settled for Rs 3/- to the Shiva Temple. He would direct him around the street to his aunt's from there. She wasn't to know the train he was coming on. It had been too short a time to reply.

The rickshaw pulled up, but Aunt, who was sitting on the verandah, didn't look up from her rice cleaning.

"Namaste, Aunty," Shiva called out as he climbed down from the rickshaw.

She looked up and smiled. Placing her winnowing cane basket down, she stood up slowly. "My knees aren't as good as they used to be I'm afraid. You know I had a feeling that you were on your way. I went to perform puja this morning. On the way out a jay bird was sitting on the lingam in the outer courtyard. It made me feel you were coming. Here you are too."

She pulled out the end of her sari and insisted on paying the rickshaw wallah. Her tone changed as she called out with an Indian woman's house authority voice: "Sughabhai, Sugha come quickly, my nephew is here."

As if by magic the girl instantly appeared. Shiva knew she had heard them and was already standing behind the front door peeping at them. She was quite tall and dark and looked old enough to mature soon, if she hadn't already. Shiva doubted though that Aunt would have a mature girl working in the house. It caused too many problems with servants having their monthly periods and not being able to do kitchen jobs. The girl carried all the things inside.

"Now you just sit here with me and tell me everything. The

girl will bring us tea and heat some water for you to bathe, after that dusty train trip. I have the upper room ready for you. And I've also made the bottom room ready in case you wish to rest there during the day. It's cooler I think. Actually I've had both rooms cleaned and ready since I wrote to your father and asked him if you could come to help me. I'm so pleased you came."

Aunt pushed two cushions to the wall and they sat cross-legged in the shade of the verandah. Aunt plied him with questions. As he answered she would interject for a clarification.

The girl came with tea, a plate of three iddlis and a small pot of ghee. She put it down next to aunt. A few seconds later she came with two glasses of water both covered with dust plates. Aunt took a spoon, broke the iddli, poured the ghee over them and handed them to Shiva. He ate while she talked.

The girl never looked at him as she came in and out with the plates and glasses. She said to Aunt, "Water is hot, will I take it upstairs?"

Aunt nodded, "And don't forget to undo the window."

An hour had almost gone since his arrival and Chinni had not appeared.

"Where's the house servant Chinni babu, Aunt?"

Aunt did a shuffle with her bottom and looked up and down the verandah. She leant forward and said, "Don't ask. Oh dear, don't ask. It's just too much to speak about. I had to send him away last month at an hour's notice. Don't ask me more. He caused me such trouble and pain. I can't bear to even think about it. The rascal. After all these years with me. Ohhh I did feel disgusted when I found out. Anyway, no more. Your bath water is ready. Go and bathe. Take rest and I'll call you later."

Shiva went upstairs and the girl scurried from the room.

He closed the door, took out the sports magazine and opened it to the middle-page poster spread. He placed it on the small table near the window.

He bathed slowly, thinking about Chinni babu. He dried and put on a lunghi and lit three incense sticks that were at the side of the deity frame on the wall. There was a small bowl of ash on the frame tray. He ran three lines of it across his forehead. He knew that it always made his aunt happy to see something on his forehead! He didn't mind going through the ritual but he disliked the smell of ash. His choice, if he had to make one, would always be sandlewood paste.

Shiva lay on the bed, the ceiling fan clicking quietly as it moved the warm air around. He was back at Aunt's after two years — lying on the same bed. But there was a big gap. The gap was that Chinni wasn't here. He felt many mixed feelings. Shiva lay on the bed all afternoon. He smiled and acted normal whenever Aunt came up to see him or talk, but he was depressed.

In the evening Aunt asked him to stay in the house, as she was going to hear the swami's discourse. She gave him a list of 'be carefuls' about this and that.

"Now if you get hungry you can take what you want from the kitchen." She pulled a large bunch of keys out from her waistband under her sari and slipped two off. One was for the kitchen and the other for the back door. "But if you wait until I come back, why, I'll serve you myself." She smiled. "I must go. I mustn't be late. Now be careful. The radio is on the shelf. You know that anyway." She picked up her torch and stick and pushed the girl along in front of her.

Shiva closed the door; he went back upstairs to his room and sat forlorn on the chair. He could only think about his last visit and Chinni Babu...

College Days

"DO YOU mind if I borrow your bike this afternoon? I have to take a note to my engineer cousin at Corot. Unless you want to come with me of course." Sam was walking across the College ground with Shiva during an afternoon change of classes.

"I'll go with you if I can come in too. I'd like to see their office. You said they have a draughtsman there didn't you?" Shiva replied.

"Sure, he works in my cousin's office. I've seen him at work when I've been before."

It was quite a ride across to the factory. The Nepalese gurka gateman recognised Sam and waved him through. Sam got a note out of his bag and they walked into the reception area. He could see his cousin at the far end of the long office. He had his own glass-partitioned cubicle. The receptionist smiled and chatted to Sam as she telephoned his cousin. Shiva could see him bending over a large model of something that looked like a piston with a pipe. Shiva watched him pick up the phone without looking away from the model; he seemed engrossed in it, even from a distance.

He looked up and waved at Sam to go down. "Come on in," he said to Shiva who was now looking carefully at a large mural on the wall.

The office was large and in one corner sat a draughtsman at a high table surrounded by retractable lights, long T-squares and lots of odds and ends that Shiva didn't recognise. Sam introduced Shiva and handed the note to his cousin who read it and sat down.

"Shiva is very interested in the draughtsman's work."

Mark, his cousin, looked up from the note. "Take him over and introduce him to Deepak. It's going to take about half an hour to get an answer for this note."

It was the best half-hour that Shiva had spent — well, at least since Ramu left! He came away with a copy of *Draftsman Lines*, a monthly magazine from the USA, and a copy of *Indian Engineers Journal*. Shiva liked Sam's cousin — a really easy-going person. Sam was not happy about the reply to the note. It meant his taking a day off from College and he was close to his limit on attendance already.

On the way home, Sam said, "I'll take you by the brothel street and show you where the best girls are. It's the middle hut with the blue curtain and the blue painted door. I tell you once you have had one or two really good fucks you won't be interested in any guy's cock. That's my opinion."

Shiva and Sam still shared everything in their lives. Shiva had to admit to himself that listening to him sometimes was very depressing, especially when Sam told him the things his father did. Last week he had bundled up whatever papers he could find in the house, including Sam's study notebooks, and sold them for waste paper. Fortunately the Muslim waste-materials dealer knew the antics of the man and waited until he saw Sam's mother going home from school and called her. She was furious and beat him with her chappal. But he just made his usual promises of 'not doing such things again'.

Sam swung off the main road down past the Revenue Office and into the street where the 'red light' houses were behind the hospital. It looked a normal street with rows of neat hutments. Several women were out in the front sweeping and others were drawing 'moogalu' designs on the ground with lime powder. It looked nothing like the pictures Shiva had seen in the *Illustrated Weekly* about the brothels in Bombay's infamous area. Sam gave Shiva their understood sign and he looked quickly to the left and saw the house. Sitting on a cot were two women cleaning rice and another standing and watering the tulsi plant in front of the house. The plant pot was painted blue too.

At the end of the street Sam casually said, "So, what's wrong with my suggestion? Why don't you just go along there one evening?"

Shiva didn't reply, he didn't know what to say, what excuse, what comment to make.

"Look if you are frightened of getting some sex disease I'll even get you a rubber, you know, a Nirodh," Sam said in a low voice.

Shiva wasn't worried about the STD problem, he just couldn't imagine going there. He felt no interest in the idea at all.

Between M.G. Road and the temple street was a small lane everyone called Dye Street because of the merchants whose shops were there. Halfway down was a small park covered in concrete, with a number of cement benches that all faced towards the centre and a statue of the Father of the Nation. Sometime since its erection Gandhi had lost his glasses and the cement walking stick had crumbled, so that all he held was a piece of cement with thin rusting rods hanging down.

Sam stopped at the park. Shiva jumped off the bar and Sam ran the bike to the wall. They went inside the park after Sam had called to the teashop wallah a few yards from the boundary. They sat down after carefully spreading their handkerchiefs on one of the benches. A small boy came quickly from the teashop with one glass of tea on a saucer. Sam poured half the tea into the saucer and handed the glass to Shiva. Sam sipped and slurped his tea from the saucer and made the boy laugh with the noises he made. Sharing one glass of tea between them was what they and many of their college friends called a 'one by two'.

When they finished the boy took the glass and saucer and with a little gesture and grin whipped a cigarette out of his shirt pocket for Sam. The boy knew Sam well. He lived in a hut just down from Sam's parents house.

"Now this is a habit I wouldn't want you to have, but once you get the taste it's hard to give it up." Sam lit the cigarette and blew a few puffs out, trying to make smoke rings, but the breeze was too strong. "Just like once you get the habit of fucking a few girls you won't want to give it up. You'll forget this other useless thing you are doing. It's boys' play. You'll see that once you have had a few really good huffings and puffings."

Shiva laughed loudly and the teaboy looked over at them to see what had happened.

Sam gave Shiva a full description of what to do. "Look I've got a hard just telling you." Sam ran his hand down his trouser fly and pressed his hard penis to the side. He looked at Shiva and smiled, "Come on what do you think?"

Shiva turned slightly to Sam and looked down at his hard bulge. He looked up at Sam and gave a certain grin. Sam raised his eyebrows. "You dirty bastard, you'll never get your hands on mine."

They laughed together. Sam knew that Shiva would like to do just that. Shiva had hinted a few times, but Sam was totally disinterested. They stood up and walked out of the park. Sam turned to the teashop and paid and walked home. Shiva rode the short distance in the opposite direction.

Shiva's mother called him as he walked through the hall and asked where he had been. He told her the truth, he just didn't tell her about the conversation! He sat in his room and looked at the two magazines he had been given. He put them to one side and opened his notebook to start his homework. He would have liked to read the magazines but knew his priority was to finish the homework assignments first.

He stopped his studies at eight and took a hot bath, went and ate supper and came straight back to study. It was too late by the time he finished to read anything else. He turned the light off and lay on the bed. All he could think about was what Sam he said and Sam's feelings when he had seen the women sitting outside the brothel. He had felt nothing. He had felt something though seeing Sam's hard bulge. In truth he was frightened that if he did go to one of the women it would be a failure. He would not be able to do it. That would be very humiliating and embarrassing. He fell asleep and woke up to hear his sister calling him. It was Saturday and only a half-day at College. He had his English assignment finished and knew they would get another one this morning. He was managing well with the English, he felt. Not as fine as Sam or his elder brother. They spoke a lot of English in their house because their mother insisted on it.

He arrived at Sam's place a few minutes early. He rode there every morning and he and Sam took it in turn to either pedal or sit on the bar holding the books. Going to College was downhill slightly and coming home was quite an effort if the wind was blowing. Sam's mother had named them 'the bicycle twins'. Shiva's father who had heard through his brother that he rode with Sam on the bicycle to College and back, made several comments about Sam not having his own bike — "If his father didn't drink so much." Shiva agreed with his father, which ended the conversation.

On the way to College, Sam, who was pedalling, said, "I just couldn't resist it last night. After passing there in the afternoon and sitting in the park talking to you I went when I had finished at the bookstore." He swerved to miss hitting a dog and stretched his foot out to give it a kick. It yelped off. "Blew five rupees and my semen like a rocket, nearly filled the Nirodh with the stuff." He laughed and nudged Shiva in the back. "I told the young woman that I might come again next week and bring a friend," Sam whispered in Shiva's ear.

Shiva felt frozen to the bar. "You didn't tell her my name did you?" he asked in an almost fearful voice that Sam knew well.

"No, of course not," Sam paused. "Didn't have to." He turned across the roundabout ringing the bicycle bell at a woman carrying a headload of green leaves heading towards the market. "She said, 'Oh I hope it's that sexy looking guy that you rode by with this afternoon'."

Sam swung round to miss another bike being ridden by an old man with a bag of something strapped on the back. Shiva was still frozen to the bar. His mouth had gone dry.

"She must have seen us. See, women think you are sexy looking — no problem, she'll really give you a good first time."

Two other students rode up beside them and the conversation turned to the College drama that was being proposed by the arts students.

On the way home with enough assignments to keep them busy the subject didn't come up. They rode all the way together with other students. The topic had changed from the drama to the student council elections next month, something that greatly interested Sam and bored Shiva.

Shiva got straight down to studies in his room. He took a fifteen-minute break and went to puja. His father made a space for him to sit next to him and gave him the bell-ringing job. He did it with indifference, just to keep things quiet between him and his father.

Shanti came to his room after he returned with a tiffin of oopma and tea. Shiva loved the way Shanti roasted the rice flour until it was almost brown and then cooked it, and he preferred her tea to anyone else's in the evening, because she always added crushed ginger. She stayed only a few minutes to gossip about nothing in particular.

Shiva heard the crowd walking down the side street, they were all heading towards the Leela Theatre he was sure. A new film was being shown tonight. He could hear people talking about the main actress. He got up and stretched. He stood quietly at the well drawing water, washing himself and listening to the people talking. He had seen the posters on the College wall, he wanted to see the film, but it wasn't the actress they were all talking about that he wanted to see, it was the hairy muscular villain that attracted him. He sauntered into the dining room, where he was the last to eat. His mother was putting things away in the kitchen. His plate was on the stool. He ate silently and took his plate out to the cleaning area. His mother told him to just leave it. As he came back she gave him a small flask that he knew was filled with hot milk.

"I'm locking up now, I'm tired. Goodnight Shiva." His mother looked tired too. He said goodnight and walked through the silent house and back to his room. He pushed his study books to one side. He brushed his hair and walked to the small narrow door in the side wall, unlocked it and pulled it open slightly. He knew how to do it so it didn't squeak. He stood there, fancying in a wild fantasy that some guy might pass by. Might stop, might come in, and might, might, might... After half an hour he went back into his room and lay down; he 'turned on the picture of Chinni', masturbated, and went to sleep.

On Tuesday afternoon coming home, Shiva pedalling, he said to Sam, "I'm not promising anything, but... and don't say anything to anyone please."

Sam turned slightly: "Listen Threado, do I ever, have I ever said anything to anyone about what we talk about? Have I, ever?" 'Threado' was Sam's special name for Shiva when he wanted to make some point. It came from Shiva wearing his Brahmin threads. It would be offensive to most people if they knew its meaning. No one else shared it though and they enjoyed such friendship. They were twins in so many ways — but certainly not identical. "So what's the big deal?" Sam added.

"Get me a couple of Nirodhs, I've never tried one."

Sam laughed quietly and Shiva nudged him. "Alright I'll get you three, but don't ask me to help you try them on, okay," Sam said and laughed again.

Shiva laughed and leaned forward. "Bad luck for me." He had

secretly thought that maybe he could get Sam to show him how to put one on. Deep down though he knew this was only a wild fantasy.

The next afternoon on the way home, Sam said, "Here." He slipped a piece of newspaper into Shiva's shirt pocket. Shiva was about to ask what it was, when three students joined them riding and started on about the student elections. It seemed that one group wanted Sam to stand for secretary. Sam was definitely Congress through and through. His useless brother-in-law was a party member and always attending some rally or other. In the talking and shouting and riding Sam said in a casual manner to Shiva, "It's yesterday's request".

Shiva thought it might have been.

The next morning Shiva nearly fainted when he called for Sam and in front of everyone he said, "Did you fill one up last night?" Shiva sat glued to the seat and his hand went tight on the tea glass he was holding. He knew exactly what Sam was referring to.

Quickly he looked up and said, "Yes, the forms were difficult to fill up, it took a little time to get it done. The first one was a mess and I threw it away. The second time was okay though. I've still got one form left. I can help you fill it up this afternoon if you want."

Sam picked up his bag of books. "Come on it's late." They laughed on and off all the way to College.

On the way home that Wednesday afternoon, riding by Abdullah's house Sam said, "Saw Abs on Sunday, he looked happy for a change. Said things were going well for him. His father is still making him travel all the way home on Thursday nights though. Said the course is pretty hard."

Everyone in their group and in the cricket team had been surprised when Abdullah told them one Sunday morning at the stadium that his father had got him a seat at the Nehru Memorial Engineering College. They knew that he had the marks, but never imagined Abdullah's father would have paid the money for the 'donation to the building fund'. Abdullah was elated beyond words in the first few minutes of his father telling him that he had been successful in getting admission. It only lasted a minute because then the rules came. Not the College rules, but his father's. He was tempted to say that he didn't want to go. But he sat and listened, nodded and bowed, agreed and felt like a child, as always in front of his father. Everyone in the house celebrated. Everyone in their community did. They all felt it was a great honour, or a great opportunity.

Abdullah did too, but the rules were so out of proportion. He couldn't share his frustration with anyone in his family or community. If he did, it would definitely get back to his father.

Sam was surprised that Shiva didn't even make a comment. "Hey, what's wrong, didn't you hear what I said? Usually when I mention Ab's name you chat on about him and nothing else for ten minutes."

Shiva turned quickly, "Sorry, I was miles away. Yes I agree, Ab looks happy. Must have a girlfriend or something over at the Engineering College."

Sam stopped pedalling, the bike freewheeled down the incline towards the rail crossing. "You reckon? He never said anything to me, what did he tell you?"

"Nothing, just a comment."

Sam started to pedal again, the bike rattled over the rails. "You might be right too. You remember a couple of months ago. It was a Saturday night. I was working, you and him went off together. Remember he said about a girl sending him a note. Maybe he wasn't joking." Sam carefully steered the bicycle around a herd of buffalo that were meandering down the road. "You remember that?"

"Watch out!" Shiva shouted. One of the buffalo had suddenly turned across the road towards a barking dog. "Sure I remember that night."

That Night

ABDULLAH HAD met Sam that evening at the Clock Tower centre and they had tea together. Then they walked down to the bookshop where Sam was working. Shiva was standing outside and asked Sam if he wanted to go to the second show. Sam said he couldn't because he had his aunt and uncle staying with them. Abdullah didn't want to go either. He wasn't in the right mood, he said in a depressing way. He wanted to talk to Shiva though. He could always confide in him and know that nothing would get back to his father.

"Come on Shiva, let's walk down to the river, I want to tell you about this beautiful girl who is sending me notes every day."

Sam looked at Abdullah, "Pig shit on you Abdullah, what a lie, the only beautiful girls in this town that write notes, write them to me."

They laughed together. Sam ran up the three steps into the

shop and Abdullah and Shiva walked off.

"What's so important at the river Abs, surely not the smell?" Shiva didn't really like walking to the river. The trees and shrubs were all surrounded by people's morning toilet offerings, and the colour of the water was brown. The smell from the tannery upstream permeated the water, and in the evening the inland breeze blew more of the tannery smell down the river. "It's more like a sewerage canal than a river."

Abdullah stopped and looked at Shiva. "Okay, anywhere, just to talk by ourselves, I've got to scream at someone or I'll go mad."

Shiva smiled and patted him on the shoulder. "I read that it's called the generation gap — they don't understand us and we don't understand them. I'm going to write a book about it, starting in chapter one with me and my father. You can have chapter two if you like."

"Oh really Shiva I get so angry inside me. My brother drinks and everyone in our house and community knows it. Does anything get said to him? No, never. But if I'm late home from the pictures I'm called a useless fellow."

They had walked along Main Road and came to the junction. They stood on the footpath, almost pressed to a building wall as a marriage procession wound its way by. There must have been four or five hundred people. They were coming from the temple. The procession was lit up by women carrying Petromax kerosene pressure lamps on trays balanced on their heads. The band was playing very traditional music.

When it eventually passed they continued slowly along the main road, chatting. When they reached the temple they turned and went down the lane at the side of Shiva's home. Shiva stopped at the small narrow gate, his 'fantasy' gate. He reached up and took an old tongue cleaner from the wall. He wiggled it through a crack in the door frame and lifted up the catch. The door in the wall opened a fraction. He pushed it and turned sideways and stepped in. Abdullah followed. They sat in his room and said nothing for a few minutes.

"Want something to drink?" Shiva asked.

Abdullah shook his head, "Just water." Shiva passed him a glass from the clay pot in the corner.

"Can you imagine Shiva I have to leave Gudur every Thursday afternoon and come home. Three hours by bus. Attend prayers on Friday and then Friday evening go back. Go to college on Saturday and then — " he paused " — then try to catch up on my studies. I'm also expected to come home every second Saturday if it's a half-day at College. The three hours on that road is bone-shaking. I can't read anything while I'm on that bus."

He stopped and drank more water. "That's not the only thing. It was also what he said about other things. He told me that he would check to make sure I was not keeping company with any students who drank. Ha, I shouldn't have to keep company with my brother! What a joke. Then he threatened me about smoking. I don't smoke and I don't like it. I told him that and then he started on 'student temptations to smoke' — wow, what a lecture!" Abdullah laughed. "He went on so long that it was stopped only by the call to prayer. I laughed to myself about it. Then, can you believe, we came home and he started where he had stopped before prayer! He took me up on the roof and said in a low voice, 'Now the greatest temptation, because you will have money, is to visit a brothel, a house of bad name'. I got the full lecture on sexual diseases spoiling me."

He paused and picked up a pencil from Shiva's table and doodled on a scrap of paper. "The real pain is that he is insisting that I will only wear, only wear, white pajamas. I'm going to look like some fanatic freak all of the time."

Abdullah leaned back on the bed against the wall. He smiled. "The only thing he didn't mention was whether I could masturbate or not."

They looked at each other and grinned. "If he thought you did," Shiva replied, "I bet you he would have banned it too."

"No question about that."

Shiva got up and unlocked the door. "I'm going for some buttermilk, want some?"

Abdullah nodded.

Shiva came back and closed the door. No one had seen him take two glasses. He didn't want anybody to know someone was in his room, and certainly not Abdullah. That would have freaked his father out. Even the thought that a Muslim might step into the house would be enough to start a major ritual cleaning.

"How often do you masturbate?" Abdullah asked as he finished drinking the buttermilk and put the glass on the floor.

Shiva had thought the bulge in Abdullah's pajamas was a bit big when he had come back with the buttermilk. Maybe it was just the cloth fold. Maybe it wasn't.

"Well if I'm not too mentally tired with study and I can think of something interesting, or someone interesting," Shiva grinned, "I

70

like to do it every day." He paused, "So how is that for an honest answer?"

"I can't believe it. I really thought you would have got angry for me even asking the question. Actually I thought it was only me that was interested in it every day. So many guys talk about it as though you will lose your power and energy, or go blind and that kind of thing if you do it. I have thought about it a lot." Abdullah sat up higher against the wall. "What about guys who are married and do sex with their wives day after day, like Yusuf next door? I hear them every night at it."

Shiva felt himself going very hard.

"Can I ask you another really private question?"

Shiva wondered quickly what it would be. Maybe he would ask how much came out or something. Whatever the question he decided he would give an honest answer. Why not? Abs had started the discussion. He smiled and nodded.

Abdullah didn't speak for a while. Then he smiled and looked at Shiva. "Well," he paused and as he spoke he put his hand out and touched Shiva's crotch, pressing slightly on his now very hard cock, "you ever do it with anyone else?"

He took his hand away. Shiva had sat still and hardly reacted.

"Yes" — and this time he stretched out his hand and placed it on the bulge in Ab's pajama pants. He felt its whole length. There was a lot of length too! "You remember my cousin Ramu. We started that time he umpired the cricket match. We do it together whenever he can come. Haven't seen him since College started."

"Ramu, wow, that guy's a hunk, really nice." Ab paused. "Let's..."

Shiva was so excited. He pulled the cord on Ab's pajamas and tugged the waistband forward and down, and almost like magic it jumped out. Shiva had never seen a hard circumcised penis before. The whole head was fully exposed and there was no loose skin.

Ab was having trouble undoing the hook on Shiva's pants. The zip had come down easy. Shiva sat upright and slipped the hook. Ab had his hand inside his underpants and squeezed Shiva's foreskin. Shiva wriggled a bit and with his free hand pulled his underpants and trousers down.

"What a weapon Shiva, it's really thick isn't it?"

In fact they were both about the same length but Shiva's was thick. He knew that his was now thicker even than Chinni babu his first guru's, and thicker than Ramu his cousin's. Shiva was rather astounded though at the size of the head on Abdullah's. It was like a large mushroom, the type that comes up after the first monsoon rains.

"I didn't know about masturbating before they circumcised me and I often wonder what it would have been like to masturbate if I still had the skin."

"The door's locked, no problem, let's take our clothing all off." Shiva wriggled off the bed and so did Abdullah. They helped each other undress, and did it rather slowly.

Ramu would certainly have sighed and groaned if he'd have been there. Ab's body was really strong and muscular, Shiva really admired him. He looked down and didn't see a hair on his chest or stomach until he came to his navel button. All around it and running down was a thick mat of pubic hair. It looked like a peepal leaf upside down.

"I think that you are going to be really hairy, aren't you Shiva." Abdullah smiled as he said it and ran his fingers straight up the centre of Shiva's stomach and chest. There was this thin new line of hair starting to grow. It was just a straight line, it didn't show across his chest. Abdullah was slowly and firmly rolling Shiva's foreskin back and forth. He put his hand under Shiva's balls and moved them around slowly. It was delightful.

Shiva rubbed his fingers all over Ab's penis, concentrating on the large head. Ab shuddered and the semen shot out onto Shiva's arm followed by another shot on his stomach. Shiva kept on rubbing and Ab grabbed his hand and doubled over. He let out a deep 'Ahh...'

Abdullah straightened up. Shiva used his T-shirt to wipe off the come. Abdullah gently pushed Shiva back onto the bed, crouched over him and masturbated him with quick changes of hand. It was driving Shiva to a pitch. Ab moved his legs so that he was now kneeling right over Shiva's cock. Shiva felt it starting to erupt and just as it blew Abdullah moved so that it blew onto his crotch behind his balls. He kept it pressed tightly there. Shiva panted and lay very still.

Ab remained crouched in the same position for a minute and then jumped off and stood up grinning. Shiva raised himself on one elbow and made a loud sighing sound. He stood up and wrapped a cotton towel around himself. He went out and wet it in the bucket and shared it to wipe themselves. They dressed and sat again on the bed.

"I suppose you will think I am mental or something, but I'd like to do that with you anytime we can. I'm away so much now, and when I do come home my family always seem to have things going on that commit me to be with them. Or more to the truth, my father makes me join in."

He paused and looked at Shiva and ran his hand across his face slowly. "I could come any Friday night. I could leave the house and come here and then catch the late bus back."

Shiva knew that he too wanted more of the same, and more with Ab. "I want to be with you like this," he paused, "and more, any time we can organise it." He sat up. "I'm home every Friday now studying. I'll leave that side gate open. All you have to do is push it and come in. That's even easier than saying we'll meet here or there and get it screwed up missing each other or running into other guys. Just come around."

Then Ab did something quite unexpected. He rolled Shiva on the bed, lay on top of him and hugged him. "I want to be with you too."

And now more than three months later, with an exam coming up, Shiva sat at his study desk, books open, but he wasn't studying. He sat watching the smoke from the sandlewood incense sticks waft slowly across the room. He had added an extra two sticks to camouflage the smell of the anti-mosquito coils his mother had insisted he use. He was thinking about the first time with Ab. It wasn't the first time that he had sat and thought of that first time, more likely the hundredth, thousandth or more. As always he remembered it in detail and each time he thought of it, he felt himself tingle inside, an urge of excitement in his groin.

He remembered this afternoon on the way home too, that Sam had said Ab looked happy. Shiva knew why. He and Abdullah shared a secret beyond anyone's wildest imagination. He knew there were lots of things that Ab was not happy about, but there was one overriding thing that was giving Ab a new happiness. He and Shiva shared that happiness between them. It had been a shared Friday night happiness almost every week since the first time. They had only not met on three Friday nights. With every second Saturday of a month being a declared holiday for government and educational institutions, they had made up for one on the second Saturday of last month. Ab's father's insistence that he come home for Friday prayer at the mosque his grandfather had built and then go all the way back

Shiva didn't know until they got talking on the Friday night that the same evening as he was sitting and thinking this, Ab was standing in the bathroom in the college hostel masturbating and thinking of Shiva. It was an incident Shiva told Ab afterwards he would never forget, which he would one day write in the epic story book of their lives. Shiva often made Ab laugh with his fantasy that one day he would write their story. It would be an example of communal harmony — the son of a fat, overbearing, tyrannical Hindu pujari, and the son of an equally tyrannical and fanatic Muslim, living openly together as men who loved men.

"Shiva, I went into the bathroom with only one idea, you know what that was, eh! To stand facing the door, masturbating and thinking of how fantastic it would be if there was a knock and I opened the door and there you were." Ab paused, grinned, sighed and went on. "Then it happened. I was just at that point of no return, you know, what you call 'execution' point. I felt this strange tickling feeling on my foot. I looked down, and there were two, not one but two cockroaches sitting on my foot, facing each other wriggling their long feeler things together. I wanted to scream, I wanted to shake my foot to get them off. But I couldn't. The feeling was already out of my balls and halfway up my cock. It blew out and one of the large blobs landed on one of them. They both fled into the drain, one after the other."

And Then There Were Three

SHIVA GOT home late from College. He had promised his mother to be home on time and hadn't meant to be late. Every Tuesday he went to cricket practice with the seniors. The Sports Master, or S.M. as he preferred to be called, was picking the Inter-College Team and he wanted to be on it. He had thought it would be great if their College was playing against the Engineering College and Abdullah was on the team.

Just as they were about to hear the preliminary selection list a willy-willy had started to blow without warning over the cricket ground. It whirled across the pitch and veered suddenly towards them all. They were on the far side of the large old banyan tree. It was strong enough to blow the students' bikes over into a tangled mess and cover them all with sand, dust and bits of twigs and leaves. The pedal of one boy's bike had knocked the chain off of Shiva's.

them all. They were on the far side of the large old banyan tree. It was strong enough to blow the students' bikes over into a tangled mess and cover them all with sand, dust and bits of twigs and leaves. The pedal of one boy's bike had knocked the chain off of Shiva's. He tried to explain this to his mother, but his father came in and shouted at him for telling such a nonsense excuse, for simply being a useless fellow and being late home.

His father went out muttering, and his mother went on scolding him, refusing to give him the samosa tiffin and tea his sister had ready for him. His sister had tried to calm her mother down a bit but it hadn't helped. Suddenly she smiled at Shiva, knowing she had remembered something that would get him out of the kitchen. "There is a letter for you on your father's chair. It has that funny drawing on it. Must be from Ramu."

Shiva knew that Shanti had given him the excuse to escape and he did so in a flash, making a quick 'namaste' sign to his mother. He often did this as he knew she saw it as a sign of his love and respect for her. Tonight though she just grunted.

He collected the Inland letter from Ramu, stuffed it into his shorts pocket and went to the outside fire to collect hot water for bathing. He could smell the willy-willy dust in his nose, and he felt grimy all over. He bathed quickly, and wrapping a clean dry cotton towel around his waist, sat on the end verandah, under the jasmine creeper. Just as he opened the letter two small white-whiskered monkeys swung from the roof gutter onto the jasmine vine. They froze for an instant on seeing him so close. They screamed together and fled back across the roof. The small white-scented flowers fell on Shiva. A few landed and stayed on the letter. He moved them around as he read. He and Ramu had not seen each other for a few months, not since College started. Ramu had been working with the Corot company for almost four years.

The first two years were great for both of them. Ramu had been sent to the Hyderabad office for management training. Every month he got six days off. When he was doing shift work at the factory he got eight days at the end of each month, and came and stayed in Chintana every time. He rarely went home because his brother constantly demanded money for something or other. Ramu gave money to his mother to help manage the house. This he didn't mind. His brother's demands were always for what Ramu considered luxuries. Things that he didn't even buy for himself.

Then Ramu got transferred to the small new factory at Nellore and although he didn't get such long breaks, he had more regular days off. He would appear at Shiva's home every ten days or so and stay three or four days. For Shiva it was just what he needed. He would have liked more. He knew more and more that he was really attracted to men. He knew also that he wasn't in love with Ramu. It was less than that. But it was a great friendship with a great physical relationship.

He wondered about his relationship with Ab. It seemed to be growing deeper than he had ever imagined it would. Shiva knew it had started as a physical attraction. Then it had slowly changed into a close and open sharing relationship. He felt that they 'knew' each other. That they were able to communicate their feelings without necessarily using words. A look, a smile, a gentle touch of fingers. He also felt that Ab was more emotionally involved with him than he was with Ab. Whatever it was at this stage he knew one thing — he was a young man who loved other men.

He felt happy, folded the letter, went inside, turned on the light, sat on his bed and read the letter again.

Dear Shivaji,
    Sorry for being so slow in writing. I really could not get to see you in the last two months as I explained in my last letters. However the Company exams are over. I passed and got my upgrade and the increase in salary — great! I am really happy about that of course.
    So, my cricket friend, I'm coming, in two weeks, second Saturday weekend. Hope you are ready and waiting for a game. I will arrive on Friday and stay just a couple of days this time. So just be patient for two weeks.
    We start our new job responsibilities early next month.
    Please give the usual greetings to everyone in the house.
    As always, N.C.

Shiva folded the letter. He knew well what the 'N.C.' stood for. Yes he would be ready for the night cobra.

Friday night, and Ab would be coming around too. Shiva sat and wondered what Ab would say to this! He knew that Ramu would be slightly jealous of the fact that he had 'discovered' Ab.

Whenever Shiva was with Ab he always thought of what Ramu had said that first time. He knew that Ramu would be very interested in a 'trio' — the question was, whether Ab would.

The evening had turned sultry, the breeze had dropped. Shiva resolutely read and answered the Civics textbook homework. He then took a cold bath. He smiled to himself: even the cold water didn't diminish his erection. He had decided to take the bath, and in getting the soap saw the little blue jar on the upper brick ledge. The sight of it made him very excited — the memory that jar contained was exciting every time he looked at it.

Last Friday, like every Friday after he and Abs 'discovered' each other, he came straight home from college. He made a point of going to puja with his father without argument. He waited until the main ritual was over and quietly slipped out. He took a hot water bath and dressed casually. He raided the biscuit tin, filled up the flask with hot milk and retreated to his room. No one disturbed him. They all just assumed he was studying harder than usual. He was studying hard too, but some time each Friday night he took a break — usually it was around nine-thirty. Last Friday Shiva didn't even hear the gate swing open. He was a little surprised when Ab appeared at the door, smiling. When they were standing naked facing each other Ab drew back, picked up his white pajama and pulled out a small round squat jar. It was blue glass.

"I took it out of my father's room. He has a box of these jars. Some Muslim medicine man sells it to him every few months. It's supposed to add vigour to your cock. I tried it a few times when I masturbated. It's nothing special I'm sure, but the feeling is good. It's kind of cool on the skin." He unscrewed the lid and held it out to Shiva. "Rub some on my knob."

Shiva had tried oil before too and liked it. He put his finger in the jar and rubbed it slowly around Ab's knob. Ab ran some inside Shiva's foreskin, then pulled the skin back slowly and rubbed even more on his 'arrow head' as Ab called it.

Ab stopped and hugged Shiva and pushed him slowly onto the bed. Shiva's legs hung over the bed with his feet just touching the floor. Ab knelt on the bed with his knees pressed against Shiva's thighs. Shiva stretched his arm out and took hold of Ab and closed his eyes. Shiva felt Ab lean forward. He had not seen the cream he had rubbed under his crotch with his finger. Shiva didn't open his eyes, but felt Ab slowly moving his cock deeper and deeper into his crotch and cheeks. Shiva knew where Ab was drawing him towards. He had never done this before. He felt a desire changing in him. Could he really penetrate into Ab? He didn't have to think because he heard Ab make a groaning noise, soft but definite. Shiva felt his arrow head penetrate.

The only thing Ab said was, "Will you?" He said it just as Shiva felt himself enter into a new experience. Ab then moved off and Shiva opened his eyes. He was putting more of the cream on Shiva's arrow head. "I know that the first time will be painful for me, but I want it. I really want you to enter me like this." He paused. "Will you?" he asked again.

Shiva just couldn't speak. He was on another planet or something. He smiled though. Ab moved back onto him and again Shiva felt himself penetrating Ab. Ab moved up and down slowly and Shiva began to move his thighs with him. He still had hold of Ab's knob and began to rub it faster. Ab moved up and down with the same movement as Shiva.

Ab let out a different groan and the semen blew as he shuddered. Shiva made two thrusts and felt himself explode inside Ab. Ab withdrew and then simply lay on top of Shiva. They both felt the semen rub between their pressing bodies. Shiva drew Ab's face closer and kissed him lightly on the lips. They were both still breathing deeply.

There was a loud clap of thunder and within what seemed like seconds rain poured down. It lasted only five minutes. They disentangled from each other when the rain stopped. Holding hands they walked out into the dark courtyard naked and washed each other. The rain started again. Ab asked if he could stay until the rain ended. Shiva said, "Wish you could stay forever."

The rain went on and on. They lay together and some time during the night came together again, laying side by side. They didn't get up and wash but lay with spots of semen scattered here and there. Shiva didn't hear Ab leave, it must have been very early morning. He slept later than usual.

"I hope you are not studying too hard," Shanti said as he came in to eat.

He smiled gently and shook his head.

The Friday of the week Shiva received the note from Ramu he waited as usual for Abdullah. He realised that Ramu would definitely come the next Friday evening or maybe in the afternoon. They were sitting together facing each other on Shiva's bed. They had their legs entwined with Shiva's under Ab's.

"Next week Ramu is coming to visit for a couple of days, what would you think if he wanted to join us, in this I mean?"

Shiva watched Abdullah's face carefully. At first it was blank and Shiva could see that Ab was at least thinking about it. He hadn't rejected the idea outright.

"Three of us. Three." Ab was almost grinning. "Ramu." He wriggled closer to Shiva, stretched out his hand and took the jar of cream off the study desk. "Rub some cream on me, slowly."

He lay down. Shiva worked one and then a second finger slowly into Ab who lay motionless with his eyes closed. Shiva then put some cream on his arrow head, his 'sticky wicket' as they called it, and moved himself forward. He moved slowly in and Ab raised his buttocks. They began to move in unison.

"Work hard on my club head," Ab said quietly. It was the first time that Shiva could remember Ab calling it a 'club head'. It was a very apt description. Shiva smiled to himself. "Ramu," Ab said. "What a great idea."

Each time with Ab was exciting. Every experience added to Shiva's feeling of what he thought he was. He had at first wondered if it all might be just a passing phase in his life. Then with his deepening relationship with Ab he knew that the feelings weren't going to pass away.

He had concentrated on looking at girls around the classroom and in the College grounds when they mixed. He liked them. He thought that some of them were really pretty. Then he would see a guy that was also attractive and the feeling came somewhere deep inside his balls. A kind of desire, an urge. He knew where his deepest attractions were. They were towards males and not females.

The week before Ramu was due Shiva concentrated extremely hard on his studies. He had to put extra effort into concentrating because if he didn't, he had fantasies. Fantasies of what it was going to be like with Ramu and Ab.

On Friday afternoon as Sam pedalled and Shiva sat on the bar Sam said, "You really seem kind of nervous or something today, what's wrong?"

"Me?" Shiva said quickly.

"No, I'm talking to the bicycle, I always do that, surely you've noticed it before!"

They laughed.

"No, nothing really. My cousin Ramu is coming and I hope there are no arguments in the house between him and his uncle. His uncle seems to have decided to dislike Ramu since he got the job at Corot."

What Shiva said about his brother-in-law was true, though it wasn't the reason why Shiva was 'nervous' as Sam called it. It was the anticipation of Ramu coming, and them being together with Ab.

He felt really excited inside his body. Shiva dropped Sam off at the bookshop where he still worked part-time. He stopped at the market corner where there were three women selling flowers, and bought two rupees' worth of jasmine. He crossed the road, got three sweets and a small bag of mixture, and dropped them in his shoulder-bag.

"Shivaji, Shivaji uncle, uncle, look Ramu uncle's here," little Venkaswamy called out from the end of the verandah. Shiva jumped off the bicycle, stretched out and grabbed the little boy and sat him on the bike seat. Ramu was sitting on the verandah with Shanti. She was trying to braid Hema's hair, but the little girl was resisting. Their father came out and told Hema to sit still. Shiva took the chance to stand up and walk inside. Ramu followed him. They walked without speaking down the passage to his rooms.

As soon as they were inside Ramu grabbed Shiva. They stood hugging each other for a minute or so. Then Ramu stepped back and sat on the stool.

Shiva took the sweets out and put them on a water tray to stop ants getting at them first. He offered some mixture to Ramu but he shook his head. Shiva placed the flowers on a clay lid and wedged the incense sticks into the Nataraj frame. He leaned against the wall.

"Well, what would you say if I told you that there are now three names?" He looked at Ramu who sat watching him and listening carefully. "You with your Night Cobra and me with my Sticky Wicket, and I've found what I will call the Club Head."

Ramu sat upright. "Go on."

"Who do you want it to be?" Shiva asked with a grin.

Ramu looked blankly. "I know who I'd like it to be." He tugged at his moustache and twisted the ends with his fingers. "The Club Head, hmm..." he put his head on one side. "If it's called that, wow, it could be. Is it Abdullah?"

Shiva pushed himself off the wall and stood in front of Ramu and placed his hands on his shoulders. "Would you like it to be, because it is?"

Ramu just stared. "You dog Shiva, it's a lie just to stir me up for tonight."

Shiva shrugged. "Well I'll tell you what, if you can wait with that cobra thing until say nine-thirty, you'll know the answer."

Ramu shook his head. "I still don't believe you."

"Okay, look in the sweet bag and see how many are there."

Ramu stood up and reached for the bag. He looked inside and his mouth fell open. "Tell me about it."

Shiva shook his head. "No, you called me a dog, so now you will have to wait. I'll tell you this much. The name fits. And he is sure interested in the three of us getting together."

Ramu leaned back against the wall and drew his legs up onto the bed. The temple bell rang.

"Come on, let's go."

Supper was rather tense that night as Shanti's husband was making comments to Ramu, until his father-in-law snapped a short sentence to shut up. No one spoke. When the patriarch got up and left, Shiva and Ramu quickly followed. Shiva went into the kitchen and asked his mother to make a jug of lime juice. She grinned at him. "You roll them first."

Shiva went over to the wire basket hanging in the corner. He took four limes and threw two to Ramu. They squatted on the floor and rolled the limes to release the juice before cutting them.

"That will do." His mother bent down and took them. They watched her cut and squeeze the limes. She added sugar to the jug and handed it to Shiva. "You add what water you want later." She jokingly pushed them out of the kitchen.

Ramu looked at his watch, nine-fifteen.

Shiva locked the door and lit another three incense sticks; he stood near the door and slowly took his clothing off. He was already hard. He walked by Ramu who just watched him. He sat on the bed holding himself. Ramu was sitting on the stool.

Ramu didn't notice it, but Shiva heard the catch. There was a quiet knock on the door, Shiva made a signal coughing sound and in walked Abs, smiling. He walked over to Ramu and put his hand on his shoulder. "Hello Ramu, hope I'm not too late."

Ramu sat glued to the stool, his mouth slightly open. Ab walked over to Shiva who was still holding himself. "You really are the sexiest Brahmin I've ever met." He leaned over and fondled Shiva's balls.

"I'm never likely to find a Muslim with a club head as big as yours."

Ramu had stood up and walked behind Ab. He wrapped his arms around Abdullah's waist, ran his hands down the front of his white pajamas and felt what Shiva had just described. Abdullah groaned and Ramu let out a soft "Wow".

Shiva pulled the cord and slipped Ab's pajama down while Ramu slipped his arms under the long white shirt and slowly raised it up and over Ab's head. Ramu dropped it on the stool. He stood there rubbing his hands over Ab's muscular chest. While Ab and Shiva slowly undressed Ramu, he made little noises while holding onto Ab's 'club'.

After a while Ramu grabbed the blanket off the bed and shook it onto the floor. Ab retrieved his shirt and reached for the cream jar. He took the lid off and held it under Ramu's nose.

"Smells good."

Ab grinned, put some on his fingers and rubbed it onto the 'cobra'. "Feels good too."

They lay on the blanket turning and changing positions until Shiva knew that it was time for Ab to get his delight. Shiva had learnt that if they played too long Ab would blow too quickly.

Ab shifted around and lay between the two of them facing Ramu, who was delighted to have the 'club'. Shiva moved slowly in and Ab groaned as always. Shiva felt Ramu sliding his hand between Ab's legs, taking holding of Shiva's balls and holding them tightly.

Later, much later, they sat and ate the mixture, drank lime juice and nibbled at the sweets. Not saying much, just all looking at each other happily.

Ab ruffled Ramu's hair as he left. He turned to Shiva, "Can we get together tomorrow too?" Ramu answered for Shiva.

Ramu and Shiva lay on the bed with a sheet drawn over them. Ramu hugged Shiva. "Happy?"

"Hhmm..."

They slept.

Birthday Gift

"IT'S YOUR birthday next month isn't it? The twelfth. A couple of weeks away?"

Sam was sitting on the bicycle bar while Shiva pedalled. It had rained last night and this afternoon on the way home from College it was still muddy here and there on the road. There were potholes filled with water. Shiva was riding slower and weaving here and there to avoid being splashed.

"Don't worry, I didn't remember it, my mom did. She writes them on her calendar. It's one of her big new year jobs."

A lorry came towards them and Shiva had to stop. Sam slid off the bar. The hutments came right to the edge of the road. It was a mud pool on the far side of the road. The lorry went by slowly avoiding a large hole in the road.

"Anyway you don't have to worry, I've already got your present."

Shiva didn't know what to say. He never expected a present from Sam, but he always got something.

"Don't worry, it's not a lunghi like last year."

They laughed at the comment. Last year's lunghi had nearly caused a riot in the house. It was bright pink and had black, red and gold dancing girls on it. The girls were very thinly clothed, in provocative positions with very large scantily covered breasts.

The day after his birthday it was something he preferred to forget. His father objected to it being so bright. His brother then started comments on the girls. One word led to another and everyone got involved.

Shiva wore it every day just to annoy those who had commented against it. He had it only two weeks and it just vanished. He couldn't find out who to blame.

The dhobi of course was the scapegoat. Shanti had said, "Can't even imagine a dhobi wanting to steal that lunghi."

"Sam, please, I know you Christians are into birthdays and that's great, but you shouldn't buy me presents."

"That's a good one Shiv, want me to make a comment about why you string wallahs don't make a deal out of birthdays."

Shiva wiggled the handlebars as a definite 'no'; he didn't want a comment. They chuckled with each other. A bullock cart was in

front and it took Shiva five minutes to get by the thing, all over-
loaded with straw. Some of it blew on them as a lorry went by
causing a draught.

They heard a train go by. "Damn, the gate will be closed."

Shiva turned at the next road crossing. They went over the
dhobi's bridge and then lifted the bicycle over the railway line. The
gate would be closed for twenty minutes and it would be choked
either side with lorries and rickshaws. The road was narrow at the
gate and like a pig's mud bath. This way would be longer but in the
end they would get home sooner.

"Want to guess what I got you?" Sam asked in a challenging
tone. "I'll tell you this much, I've already got it and I can't take it
back. I'll even give you a clue. You can't take it home."

Shiva laughed. "No, I'm not going to guess, it will take the
birthday surprise away from it."

Silence. Sam knew that Shiva would definitely try to guess in a
few minutes.

"I can't take it home with me."

Silence.

"You just won the U.P. Lottery and you got me a bull elephant
with a big cock."

Silence.

"I can't take it home with me. Sure you couldn't buy a cinema
ticket that far in advance either."

Another silence as they rode along.

"Simple, you bought a meal ticket to that old leaf-plate Brahmins' Hotel. Sure if you pay in advance you wouldn't get a refund."
They laughed and Sam shook his head.

They had come close to the Government Hospital and there
was a demonstration going on out the front. A large crowd with
banners shouting.

"Stop, Shiva," Sam said suddenly. Shiva had no option, Sam
was sliding off the bar. He squeezed the handbrakes. They walked
by the crowd that was lined up right along the wall to the corner.
Shiva got ready to ride on and nodded to Sam. Sam walked a short
distance on and stopped.

"I'm glad that protest group was there. It made it easier for me
to get you to stop. I didn't want you to hear what the present is
while you were in charge of my safety riding that machine."

Shiva smiled. He was accustomed to Sam's comments and enjoyed them.

"You can't take it home because I've already paid for it. I bought you a fuck." He pointed down the side street that lead to the houses of the prostitutes they had ridden past some months earlier.

"What's that book of records people try to get their name into?" Sam asked as Shiva stood still as the Gandhi statue on its pedestal a few yards away. "I'm thinking of sending it in under 'Birthday Gifts' or at least I could get a certificate from some government babu for creating communal cooperation."

Sam was delighted that he had Shiva still rooted to the road gripping the bike and just staring down the side street. "I can just read it now, 'Christian College Student Awarded Certificate of Merit for Promoting Goodwill Between Thread Wallahs' or..."

Sam couldn't continue, he was laughing so much; Shiva had unfrozen and was grinning at him and shaking his head in unsure belief — or unsure disbelief.

Just then Mr. D'Souza the Sports Master came along and stopped his bicycle. "You two going into the centre? I need one of you to help me please. One of the hostel boarders has hurt his leg."

II. Young Arun

Beginnings

RAMESH MUDDLI was a self-made man. At ten years old he started work with a cycle mechanic on the corner nearest his home. Two years later he became a labourer to a brick mason. His house was a small mud-brick two-roomed place with palm leaves for the roof. His father was a hard working, hard drinking rickshaw wallah who gave them all a slap in rotation when he had more to drink than usual.

His mother was a small simple woman who often got casual work as a daily coolie in the cotton godown.

Today on that small plot stood one of the best maintained small temples to Shiva in the district. It was a showpiece in so many ways. It was mainly a showpiece for Ramesh to his success. He had built the temple when his first son Arun was born.

His success was due first of all to the master mason he had served under. At twenty-two years of age his master was very proud of Ramesh's ability to lay a straight line faster than any other mason in the town. He wasn't paid anything extra for it, but he did receive twice a year a small envelope with a cash gift inside. It wasn't lavish, but that small sum went into Ramesh's Post Office Savings Account. The master gave all of his workers clothing twice a year, and Ramesh made these two sets of clothing see him through. He never bought more than a cotton towel for himself. He also worked every Sunday from the time he was eighteen, pulling his father's rickshaw. That money too he saved.

The Catholic priest in charge of St. Thomas's College had just decided to give the new contract for the compound wall to Ramesh's master when something strange happened. The mason was standing on the roof of the new Dhobhi Colony Municipality School with the Municipality Engineer, getting a certificate for payment. The clouds were rolling across the sky and the town was anticipating the first monsoon rains after a long and hot dusty summer. The Engineer said that all of a sudden the wind started to blow. They turned to climb down off the roof when the mason groaned and fell. He hit his head on the protruding window lintel and was dead when they got him to the hospital. The monsoon started at the same hour. It rained continuously all night and all of the next day. On the second morning the rain stopped for a brief hour and the cremation took place with only a few people there.

The mason's wife knew nothing about the business. Ramesh hardly knew her. After the cremation he bathed and dressed in what he called his 'cinema dress' — the clothing he kept for going out. It was the last gift of clothing from his master. He went to the widow and although she had family all around her he got to speak to her for just a few minutes.

Ramesh was friendly with their eldest daughter, the mason's favourite. She knew Ramesh as he often came in the rain to collect the tiffin box for lunch if they were working too far from home for the mason to return to eat. The daughter herself sometimes came with it and always stood and talked to her father. She was a friendly girl who had gone to school for six years.

Ramesh told the widow that unless he took on the College compound wall contract they would all have financial problems.

His next business was at the Municipality Engineer's office. He waited for the Engineer's peon to leave the room. "The masons and mason's labourers in the town are going to agitate because they feel you had somehow something to do with our mason's falling."

Ramesh stood close to the edge of the desk. The Engineer looked up with his mouth open.

"Better you make a cash payment, for all work done, and a ten per cent advance, to the widow today and I'll see that no one raises the agitation. She will take over the contract and I will supervise and do the work."

He paused and came closer to the Engineer. "I'll even make sure that she pays you the ten per cent agreed upon."

The Engineer met Ramesh at seven p.m. as arranged, and with the cash. Ramesh signed the mason's name on the voucher receipt. He counted the money, and went to the widow's house.

Ramesh had not expected the priest to be so easy to convince. He had this fear about such people, even more so when he knew they were from Kerala.

The wall took four months to finish and he gave half the profit to the widow. The priest was delighted because he thought he had got something for nothing in the extra gate-work and the watchman's small duty box. Ramesh had made his own profit with the old mason's trick.

Two years later he married the mason's daughter and started to build a small house on a piece of land he had purchased from the profit of the wall.

The Municipality Engineer was a good friend to Ramesh. They both gained well from the friendship. Other masons soon learnt that most of the brick work and construction done by the College went to Ramesh. Ramesh always gave the biggest prize donation to the College for the Students' Prizegiving Day.

Arun went to the English-medium school that the Catholic sisters ran. He knew that he had a seat in the Catholic High School and that one day he would go to their College.

Arun was at times proud of his father and at times a little embarrassed by things he did.

Arun was the first boy in his year to have a bicycle to ride to school.

When he went to the High School his father added an extra room to their now already large home. It was a separate bedroom for Arun so that his two sisters and younger brother didn't disturb his studies. That year his father also started to give him charge of all the daily payments and accounts. It was quite a burden on him with the school work and homework. Arun was popular with the other students, though not a leader.

Arun only had one fear. With all of the studies and the extra time he needed to do his father's accounts, how was he going to play hockey? Hockey was his favourite over everything else. He would find five minutes here and five minutes here and organize the houseboy Krishna to run with him around the vacant land his father owned next to their home. Krishna had never played a game of hockey but he didn't mind running with and against Arun. He thought it a bit stupid to waste one's energy chasing a ball. His sport was to sleep whenever he could find an excuse and a quiet place away from Arun's mother who had endless jobs to be done.

The Sports Master was Mr. D'Souza. He had been at the College for years. He had a two-room self-contained cottage at the end of the boarding-school building. As well as being the Sports Master has was expected to care for any of the boarders who were sick at night when the nurse was off duty.

Mr. D'Souza spoke the fastest English any of the students had ever heard. He came from Goa. He played cricket and hockey and indoor badminton in the monsoon season. He often coached the girls basketball team for the sisters. No one called him Mr. D'Souza. In fact he only answered to 'S.M.' — short for Sports Master. He was a tall strong man with a neatly trimmed beard.

Fifty first-yearers applied to play hockey for the School. Two teams were needed. The best of the players from these two teams might be lucky enough to get into the Inter Team.

Four afternoons a week for two weeks he had all fifty run, jump, leap over low hurdles and play a wild no-rules game. Five boys dropped out. S.M. then announced two teams. Arun got into Hawks as centre. By the end of the first year they were a well-knit team that challenged the second-year second team and narrowly lost in the last few minutes of the game.

Arun had counted the second-year team and only two of them didn't already have quite a lot of hair on their legs. Three had really clear moustaches and one had actually hair on his chest. He was the son of the Punjabi spare parts shop owner. His father came to all of the match games to watch his son Tippu play.

Arun's closest friend at High School that year was John. John lived near the Municipality Market in a line of houses commonly known as Christianpet. His mother was a teacher. They both liked hockey and both were excited for each other to have been selected in the team. John played wing. Neither Arun and John had even the slightest sign of dust on their upper lip.

Arun's other close friend was Pradeep, a non 'hockey wallah', and he already had a fine beginner's line of a moustache. Arun and John had to constantly listen to Pradeep and his thoughts on why hockey was dumb and cricket the 'in' game. All went to science and maths tuition together at Mr. Subbha Rao's house at six-thirty a.m. Mondays to Fridays.

The monsoon of that year was a time of excitement for Arun.

One Thursday afternoon with a dark cloudy sky overhead, the Hawks played the Eagles hockey and lost dismally. In the last fifteen minutes the rain had pelted down and the ground was muddy and slippery.

On the way home, wet and cold, John said, "Ganga is the dumbest hockey player sometimes. See the way he let them pass that goal down the centre. He would have done just as good if he had been standing there handpumping himself as waving the hockey stick around like a girl."

Arun waved as John and Ramana turned right at the junction. It wasn't the first time that he had heard both John and Ramana make comments about handpumping. He didn't know what it really meant but he had the idea it was something to do with your penis and sex.

Just as he went to wheel his bicycle across the cement walkway that covered the drain in front of their house, he slipped. He was down the embankment just saving the bicycle from going into the water. He crawled slowly up pulling the bike with him. He had to be careful as the mud was extremely slippery. The electricity went off. It was pitch dark. He saw lights appearing in the house, and knew they were lighting candles. Several flashes of sheet lightning helped him to see the walkway. Luckily the gate was open. He called out to his mother as he walked around to the back verandah, and leant the bicycle against the wall.

His mother shouted out that she had hot water for him to bathe with. Krishna ran onto the verandah with the milk as Arun scraped mud off his feet. Arun looked at Krishna, they smiled at each other. "When you take the milk into the kitchen, bring the hot water bucket Krishna, we can have a bath, you are as muddy as me."

Krishna laughed a cold laugh. "The stupid buffalo went out into that back drain just as I was ready to milk her. Then while I was milking her, the calf wandered out into the drain too."

He came out with the bucket of hot water and Arun pulled two large cotton towels from the line. They walked quickly along the side of the house protected from the rain by the roof slab overhang. Krishna was taller than Arun. Arun had always thought that maybe Krishna was maybe one or two years older than him. He had once asked Krishna how old he was, but he said he didn't really know. They poured the hot water into the large bathing water tank.

It was still very hot though. They stood naked, scraping mud off their legs and waiting for the water to cool. They looked at each other more than usual. It wasn't often that they bathed naked together. Krishna tended to always tie his shirt through his string waistband and tuck it into the back of the string after pulling it between his legs. Today his shirt was too muddy and it was also wet and cold.

Krishna grinned as he said to Arun, "You've got more hair than me now haven't you?" He was brushing his pubic hair down as he said it.

Arun looked down at his hairs and smiled back, "Hmm, and more hair on my legs. You should see Tippu though, he already looks like a little Punjabi bear."

As Arun said this he felt his penis going hard. "It's getting big too," Krishna said and laughed. His was half hard as well.

Arun squatted down and poured hot water over himself slowly. "Krishna, do you know what handpumping means ?"

Krishna was now squatting too, on the other side of the water tank. "Yes, sure. I thought you knew too."

Arun wiped the water from his eyes and shook his head in a negative answer.

There was a bang on the wall from the next room, and a muffled: "Arun hurry up your father is home he wants the wages book and the bricks order books."

It was his mother.

Arun finished bathing and dried himself quickly. He would have to go to his room, dress and get into the house smartly. His father got bad tempered having to wait for the business books. He wrapped the towel around his waist. Krishna was putting their muddy clothing into the bucket. He smiled, stepped quickly towards Arun, and rubbed his hand quickly on Arun's penis, which was still quite hard. He said quietly, "If it's still raining tonight I'll come and sleep in your room, it's leaking in the storeroom."

Arun didn't know why, but he felt somehow excited by the way Krishna had rubbed him.

Krishna loved to go into Arun's room. The walls were all covered in posters of different sports people, mostly men. On one wall was a large print of Lord Krishna and the Milkmaids. It had small coloured electric lights around the edge of the frame and a shelf that Arun kept flowers on. The room always smelt of incense sticks. On the floor was a soft Kashmir-type mat that was so nice to rub your feet on. Arun also had a big mirror and Krishna could stand for ages in front of it combing his hair into different styles.

The rains kept on and then even more thunder and lightning. His father was in a bad mood, the brick wall his masons had finished plastering at the College had been completely spoilt by the sudden storm. Just as they finished eating the lights went out and the girls made little screams as their younger brother made frightening noises until their mother shut them up. Arun lit the kerosene lamp for them. He took two candles and a matchbox and ran down the verandah to his room at the end. He found two mosquito coils and lit them and the candle. He kept his blanket and sheet in the wooden box under the bed. He was just pulling them out when the door opened quickly and Krishna stepped in smiling. He had a small tiffin carrier in his hand. "Some curried nut mixture your mother sent." He put it down on the desk.

With the candle burning on the far side he could see all different shadows in the mirror. Arun spread the sheet out and sat on the bed. They chatted for a while about different things that had happened during the last week.

"You want me to show you what handpumping is?" Krishna asked in a slightly lowered voice.

Arun raised his eyebrows and smiled. "Sure."

Krishna stood up and leaned over and clipped the bolt on the door.

They both had on lunghis; Krishna hitched his up and Arun stared directly at his much bigger hard cock. Krishna made a sign to Arun and he lifted his up too, so that his own hard erection flicked against his belly. Krishna had taken hold of his own cock and was running the skin up and down slowly. Arun tried to draw the skin back like Krishna but it was painful.

"Do you know what will happen soon?" Krishna asked.

Arun shook his head.

"Well the stuff that goes into a woman to make a baby comes out."

Arun looked at him and realized that he was talking about semen. He had read the word but never realized the significance of it. Suddenly things changed. A very different feeling started to come into his penis. Strange and exciting. He looked up at Krishna who was intent on doing the same.

"Keep going, don't stop," Krishna said intently.

Arun felt his legs tense and a deep inner drive to keep on. Without warning an even newer sensation roared through Arun and he felt the deepest most exciting feeling of his life. He glanced quickly at Krishna and as he did so a white liquid shot from his friend. Some went on the bed and some onto his leg. Then with a final ecstasy Arun saw the same fluid catapult out from himself. He shuddered and lay back on the bed. He was speechless. Krishna lay back beside him. A silence of adventure filled the room.

"And that's what they call handpumping," Arun said quietly.

"And that's what they call handpumping," Krishna copied him, turning his head and smiling at Arun.

"Should we wash it off?" he paused as he asked Krishna the question. "It's really clean though isn't it?"

This was a question Krishna had thought about several times. "It's not like piss or saliva or the stuff from your nose. This is the pure stuff that makes babies and —" he paused, "well I reckon that it's super clean." He put his hand down and rubbed the liquid over his leg.

Arun stood up and blew the candle out. His legs felt as though they had played two hockey matches in one day.

They lay on the bed together and without a word fell asleep. The rain kept on throughout the night.

Arun knew that the next day at school he had listened to the teachers and made notes, but not much had really sunk into his head. He looked around the class quietly at the other guys. He wondered who else knew about this. Maybe they all did. Lots of them made comments about it. Maybe he was the last one in the whole class to learn!

That evening he concentrated carefully on his studies. He didn't leave his study desk until called for supper. His younger brother kept him in the front room after supper for fifteen minutes asking help with his homework.

He stood and stretched himself and said goodnight to his mother. His father was still out somewhere. He closed the back door and walked along the verandah.

Krishna was locking the side gate. Arun walked over: "Will we do it again tonight?"

Ten minutes later Krishna came into Arun's room. They sat and ate the rest of last night's curried nut mixture. Krishna stood up and pulled his lunghi off. His cock was already standing up hard. Arun wanted to lean over and grab it, but Krishna moved away and turned the light off. In the sudden darkness Krishna walked towards the bed and bumped into Arun, who was sitting on the edge of the bed; he put his hand out and felt Krishna's legs. He ran his hand up the inside of his legs and felt his balls. They were not hanging freely but were tight inside their little bag. Arun ran his hand along Krishna's hard shaft. It really was big, Arun thought. Krishna drew back and leaned over and pushed Arun's legs onto the bed and they lay side by side facing each other. They ran their hands over each other's bodies.

Krishna started to handpump Arun but Arun withdrew his

hand. "It's really painful when you try to pull the skin back like that Krishna. Mine is really tight, not like yours."

Krishna took it again in his hands and holding it with one hand put his other index finger down inside the foreskin. "Mine was tight at first too. I put my finger inside like this and after a few weeks it stretched a bit and now its o.k."

Arun said nothing. He was filled with an even newer feeling, an even newer excitement, an even newer realization. It was the excitement not of handpumping himself, but of Krishna doing it to him. Even greater pleasure was the fact that he was doing it for Krishna. He had hold of someone else. How many nights in the last year, or longer, had he dreamt of doing this! In fact ever since he first started to see pubic hair growing, when he held his hard penis and squeezed it, he would dream about holding another friend's hard cock.

He had dreamed of what Krishna's was like when it was hard, and now he knew. He had held it. He had held his balls too.

In the dark Arun smiled. Krishna was a great guru. In thinking all this he wondered who had been Krishna's guru. He was going to ask him but the words didn't come out. His mouth was dry and the feeling intensified. This time it was he who blew it out first and he knew it must have landed on Krishna. He felt Krishna tense and then Krishna's fluid fell on him.

He moved closer to Krishna and hugged him to his body. Neither remembered going to sleep. Krishna must have woken up during the night because Arun found himself covered with the sheet and blanket when he woke with the alarm clock at five-thirty. They both got out of bed quickly and went their ways.

On Saturday afternoon at five Arun's father asked him, "You've done the weekly cash book, have you finished your homework?"

Arun looked up from the small table in the front room where he was at that moment doing the cash book. "No, I'm doing it now and my studies later."

"Well you can go to the cinema tomorrow, as you haven't finished, but we are all going to the first show, this evening." His father looked at his watch, and added, "In twenty minutes if your sisters are ready."

He had raised his voice as he said it. The girls heard him. His brother knew not to dare smile at Krishna, but his two sisters waited until their father had left the room.

"Bad luck the homework isn't done. We did ours correctly

when we came home from school," the younger one squeaked.

"Never mind elder brother, you can go tomorrow. Of course tomorrow's Sunday and it will be so crowded you might not even get a ticket." His elder sister said this as she took the younger one by the hand and left the room quickly.

Arun was always being poked with comments from them. He was glad he had his own room. As he thought that he smiled, he was very very glad he had his own room.

He knew what the new film was, he had seen the posters that morning on the billboards. John, Pradeep and Ramana had both commented on how big the breasts were on the poster picture of the heroine. They all agreed that the hero was a great actor. Arun looked at the villain though. He was standing with his legs apart holding a rifle in one hand and a rose in the other. That's who he would be watching mostly, Arun decided. He looked super.

Arun's mother came in. "Are you waiting for us for supper or will you eat early?"

"I might study late. Maybe I'll sleep too. I'm not sure."

She smiled and put her head to one side, saying "Students!" then raised her hands and left the room.

He heard his father at the gate: "Krishna you go in the rickshaw with the girls, we are going on the motorbike, you can come back and go with Arun tomorrow."

Arun hadn't thought Krishna would have to go with his sisters in the rickshaw. He would be back in twenty minutes or so. Arun's question to himself was, could he wait twenty minutes. He was already having the feeling. His cock was hard and he had one hand on it as he entered the bills in the cash book.

Krishna came whistling in through the gate and tapped on the door. Arun looked at the clock on the wall — twenty-three minutes. He stood up and pressed his erection down a little so it wasn't sticking out too much. He unbolted the door and Krishna stepped in and ran his hand straight onto the bulge in Arun's shorts.

"Thought so."

Arun looked down at Krishna and saw the same type of bulge and said "Thought so."

Krishna bolted the door and crossed the room to the cassette player. He put on a tape and turned the volume down a little. Arun's sisters always listened to it full blast. It annoyed their mother.

"I put water on the fire to boil, want to bath?"

"Yes, let's."

Arun was excited at that idea. It had started off with them having a bath and it had been interrupted. Now they could take a bath and maybe do it while they bathed.

And they did. They soaped each other slowly in turn and then poured water over each other. Krishna turned Arun around and slipped his hard cock between Arun's legs and moved slowly for a few minutes. He turned Arun around and Arun took both his and Krishna's cocks in the one hand and squeezed them together. Krishna had a pot of warm water and he poured it down their stomachs. They watched the soap run out of their pubic hairs. Krishna poured more water.

Then out of his fantasy of the last few nights came the urge to make it a reality. Arun bent down and put Krishna's tense cock in his mouth and drew it in and out slowly. Krishna made a sighing sound and then tried to pull Arun's head away. He had hold of his hair. Arun felt the hair being pulled but he kept on and suddenly Krishna loosened his grip, his legs bent slightly and Arun felt it fill his mouth. It tasted a bit salty. He withdrew and let the semen run out of his mouth and onto the floor.

He washed his mouth and stood smiling at Krishna, who was leaning against the wall.

Arun moved closer and turned his back to him and Krishna wrapped his arms around him and cupped his balls in one hand and masturbated him with the other. Slowly, very slowly. Pulling the skin back just to the point of pain for Arun. Arun had his eyes closed. He couldn't do anything but sag onto Krishna, as his legs went weak and it came out more than ever before. Three times it shot out like some kind of rifle.

They were in the bathroom together, bathing and drying and talking for another half hour. It took that long because Arun had asked Krishna a question and Krishna was telling him the answer. Arun could feel his eyes getting wider and wider. He knew his mouth had been half open in astonishment several times. The question had been so simple, but the answer... The answer was like a Hindu saga.

"Krishna, if it was you who taught me this, who taught you?" Krishna was half playing with running water over his face. He gurgled a mouthful and spat it out into the drain in the bathroom.

"Maybe I taught myself!" He poured more water over his face and gurgled.

Arun stretched his hand out and grabbed a few hairs. Krishna jumped.

"Tell me the truth or I'll pull them all out one by one."

They laughed together.

"That wouldn't take long with the few I've got, but if I had to do that to you, well it would take years. You've already got enough to stuff a pillow with."

"We keep secrets don't we? Well this is a real kind of secret. I suppose you will believe me."

He was still very hard and had squatted on the floor. He poured hot water on the floor and sat down on the cement. He held himself and slowly started to masturbate. Arun did the same. Krishna took hold of Arun's hand and placed it on his cock. Then he took the soap and started to rub it slowly over Arun.

"You remember last year when your cousin was here. What was his name?"

"Ashok."

"You and him were playing hockey and I ran between you to grab the ball and his stick hit me in the knee."

Arun nodded.

"That night I could hardly walk and your father asked me to take some papers down to the Father at the College. It took me ages to find him. I asked the Sports Master and he told me where to find him. He also asked what was wrong with my leg and I told him."

Krishna poured water over Arun and Arun started to rub soap over Krishna. Arun was enjoying feeling Krishna's hairless legs and Krishna had been curling the hair on Arun's leg as he ran the soap down.

"I found the Father and thought that S.M. might have some ointment for my knee. Everyone says he is good with bones and things. I stopped at his room. I knocked but heard the sound of him bathing. I waited and he then came out. I told him my knee was very painful. He took me in and I sat on the edge of a bench. He felt my knee and said I should have some ointment and a bandage."

"Yes, I remember that, you had a bandage on it for days didn't you? Yes, and that oil smelling like tulsi."

Krishna nodded. "He told me to take my lunghi off, I had my shorts underneath. He started to massage my knee very carefully and then my leg. He told me the ointment would make it feel hot."

Krishna stopped speaking, and Arun stopped listening, they knew they were both getting to the point when they couldn't stop stroking each other.

Krishna had both hands on Arun's cock, one gripping it and

the other working over the exposed knob. The foreskin was pulled as tightly back as Arun could bear. The feeling was unexplainable. He felt the semen coming and, for a second, stopped handpumping Krishna. He couldn't do anything but sit there. It flowed out and he doubled over as Krishna ran his fingers over the knob. That feeling after coming was what he called 'screaming point'. Krishna had all of the semen in his hand; he rubbed it on his own cock and within twenty movements up and down his gushed out too. They stood up and finished bathing, not speaking. Krishna knew though that Arun was waiting for him to continue. They wrapped the towels around themselves, ran inside to the middle room and sat on the large cot.

"As soon as he started to rub the oil on my leg, on this upper part," Krishna pointed to his inner thigh, "well I got hard. He said nothing, but he must have seen it. I mean it wasn't as big as it is now, but it was big enough to see sticking up in my shorts."

They laughed quietly and Arun made a 'up' sign with his finger under the towel.

"He did the bandage and then walked into his bathroom. I heard him washing his hands. The oil was feeling really hot on my leg by then. He came out and said, looking at my shorts I was sure, 'You want me to rub that for you too?' Well I smiled and said, 'No not with that oil, it might burn it off.' He laughed when I said that. He came over and sat on the edge of the cot next to me. He ran his hand across my hard thing. He took my hand and placed it on his. It was not just hard, I tell you Arun it was like a Nandi bull's stone cock in the Shiva temple."

They laughed again and Arun got up. He almost ran out and came back with two glasses of water. "Really Krishna, I'll..." he paused, "I'll cut your balls out if this is just a story. I can't believe it."

Krishna shrugged and said nothing.

"Go on."

"Go on!" he exclaimed. "Why should I go on if you don't believe me and threaten to cut my valuables off."

He sat and clutched his hands over his testicles and they grinned at each other. "Really I know. I couldn't believe it. It was such a good feeling though, that I said nothing. He then flicked my penis out and — well, just imagine."

He grinned at Arun, who asked, "What did you do to him.?"

"Nothing, all I could do was hold him. I had so much feeling in me that I sat there. I thought I must have died and found some new life or something. The feeling was, well you know what I mean now too don't you?"

Arun smiled and nodded.

Krishna got up, went out, and came back quickly with two more glasses of water. "He told me what it was and everything. Then he did it to himself." He paused, "Well you know what. I held his marbles. They are so big." He paused again, "And I ran my hand up and down his hairy chest. He is really a body builder isn't he?"

Arun was just staring at Krishna in astonishment. "S.M., wow, I would never have guessed him doing anything like this. Never." He didn't tell Krishna that he had often looked at S.M. and secretly admired his body. It was so muscular. So strong.

From that day on he would look at S.M. whenever he saw him and think of Krishna's experience. He watched S.M. as he practiced hockey with them in his shorts and would visualize his hard Nandi bull. Some nights he would lay on his bed and imagine that it was him that had the injured knee, not Krishna who had the experience.

Hyderabad

REVISION CLASSES had started. There were only a few weeks to the public exams for tenth class. Arun knew that he would pass. He had been in the top ten ranking at every exam in High School. Still he felt nervous about it. The nervousness was like a virus, passed from one student to the other. John was round at Arun's studying with him almost every night.

When John wasn't there, Arun was at his place and John's mother bombarded them with English questions. She didn't speak as fast as S.M., but her questions were always hard. If John complained, she just scowled and said, "Shut up student, I'm the examiner" and waved an imaginary stick at them both.

She always produced some interesting tiffin for them to eat. John's older brother Samuel asked them twenty true or false questions on science every time he found them together. He made some of the questions quite tricky and shouted if either gave a wrong answer — he called them 'tenth-class HPs'.

Many times Arun had thought about asking John if he handpumped very much, or if he had ever handpumped with another boy. He always hesitated though. He never quite had the courage to make the words actually come out. He had looked a hundred times towards John's crutch, but never seen even the slightest bulge in it.

Three days before the exams Pradeep came round to Arun's room where he and John were studying. Pradeep was extremely happy. "My dad just drew his number in the Chit Fund, and got the interest bonus. He says that I can go to Hyderabad for four days and see the Salan Jung museum and things if I can find some friends to go with, what do you think?"

John looked up, keeping his finger on the maths line he was questioning Arun on. "Great, only problem for me is that I don't have any money, sorry."

"Where would we stay?" Arun asked.

"My Gran has a big house in Hyderabad, we could stay there, she lives with her sister and two servants. She is always happy if someone visits her."

They talked about it and John agreed that he would go if Arun could pay. Arun often paid for things with John. They both knew and accepted their families' different financial positions. Arun's father thought it was a good idea. He spoke to Pradeep's father to make sure it was alright, then booked their train tickets. He insisted on buying all three boys a pair of pants and a shirt each.

Sometimes Arun thought that his father went to extremes.

They met at the railway station on the Monday after the exams, all confident that they had passed. John's brother Sam was there and carried a shoulder bag of sweets that their mother had cooked for them.

"What you guys need to buy is a camel, just to cart your gear around." Sam was really an actor. He made a real drama of carrying the shoulder bag as they walked along the platform.

Arun's mother had made peanut and rice puffed balls as well as rice biscuits. Pradeep's father laughed at the great quantities of food. "Hyderabad isn't under siege you know. Still my mother will help you eat them."

It was early summer and the train was crowded. Three Punjabi wallahs were trying to wedge them out of their reserved seats. Pradeep got into a loud argument with them, and several older passengers joined in. The Punjabis split up, but one remained on one of their upper reserved bunks until the ticket collector told him to shift at nine p.m. when he checked the tickets. The Punjabi guy just smiled, shrugged his shoulders and picked up his bedroll and walked to the end of the carriage. After the ticket collector left, he unrolled his blanket on the luggage shelf.

Arun had one top-tier bunk, Pradeep the opposite top-tier, and John the middle bunk below Pradeep. They changed around at the request of an elderly couple and a mother with her small child. Arun lay with his eyes closed, but sleep didn't come. He was excited about seeing Hyderabad. He turned on his side, John and Pradeep were asleep. Pradeep was almost snoring.

When the train stopped at the next station, Arun got down from the bunk and walked along the corridor to the door. It was a small station and the train only stopped two minutes. A gentle breeze was blowing in. The Punjabi had jumped down and filled his military-style water bottle. He ran back to the train as it started, and Arun stood to one side of the door, holding the aisle bar. The train gave a shudder and chugged forward. The Punjabi stood in the doorway, holding the door grill and sipping slowly from the water bottle. He moved away and Arun turned to stand full into the doorway, gripping the bar.

The Punjabi guy was tall and Arun stood wondering about him. Arun had noticed his chest, it was really hairy. Arun wondered how old the guy was. It was so hard to tell these Punjabis' ages.

He was leaning slightly out of the door, enjoying the wind blowing on his face as the train sped along. He didn't hear the Punjabi come back. He pulled himself back as he realized the guy was standing there. He turned and the guy smiled at him. Arun smiled back and moved slightly to the side, holding the door grill. The Punjabi guy stood next to him holding the aisle bar.

He spoke in Hindi to Arun, and Arun answered in his schoolboy Hindi, which seemed to make the Punjabi smile. Arun knew that he could have shifted away further from the doorway, but he didn't. He was enjoying the fact that the Punjabi had his arm slightly pressed into his crotch. Arun could feel his cock going hard.

The movement of the train added to the Punjabi's arms moving too. Well maybe, Arun wasn't sure. As the train blew its whistle and crossed through a level crossing at a slightly slower speed, Arun was sure that it wasn't just the train movement!

They had to shift a few minutes later as a little boy, half asleep, wanted to go into the toilet next to the door. The Punjabi walked over to the other side of the carriage and stood at that door, looking out. Arun decided he would stand next to him again. Why not, he was enjoying it. It was rather exciting, and anyway he wasn't feeling sleepy. This time however it was the Punjabi who stood slightly to the side. Arun leaned slightly out of the door, just as the Punjabi had. He just stood there. The guy did the rest! He moved slightly back and forth and Arun could feel the hard cock brushing back and forth across his arm.

The little boy came out of the toilet, and the Punjabi looked at Arun, smiled and nodded. Arun nodded back. They crossed the corridor and went into the toilet together.

Within seconds Arun realized that the Punjabi was an expert at this. He had his pajamas undone, down and off, slung over his shoulder. Arun had his belt undone and was about to undo the zip. The Punjabi took over.

As soon as he had Arun's pants and underpants down, he crouched and started to suck him. Arun pulled back, he was too excited and would come quickly if the guy kept the sucking up. The guy stood up and Arun took hold of his cock. It was an incredible size. Arun wrapped his fingers around it at the base. It was as thick as Arun's wrist! The Punjabi put his hand on Arun's head and lowered it to his cock. It filled Arun's mouth. The Punjabi had hold of Arun's cock and was stroking it. Then Arun felt the guy's hand running over his buttocks. Before he realized it the guy tried to put his finger inside his anus. The feeling was all too much. Arun felt himself starting to explode, and the Punjabi was going tense as well. They blew together. Arun pulled his mouth away, but not quite quickly enough. It hit his forehead and cheek. The guy smiled and used his pajamas to wipe Arun's face. Arun stood there in stunned delight.

The Punjabi was very quick, he was out of the toilet in a minute. Arun stood there for a while, slowly doing his pants up, then washing his hands and face. He was stunned with excitement. He walked slowly back to his bunk. The Punjabi was up on the goods compartment shelf, eyes closed as he walked by.

Arun looked at Pradeep and John as he climbed up onto the bunk again. They were both sound asleep. He had been up, had a fantastic sexual adventure, and, well... that was life, he thought. He lay there for a few minutes, thinking about it all, feeling very happy and content.

The train arrived three hours late. John and Pradeep tried to get Arun up, but he told them with a smile to just leave him. They made a few comments and let him stay on the upper bunk, sleeping.

Pradeep phoned his grandmother and told her that they had

arrived. He wanted to take an auto to the house. His grandmother insisted that they wait and she would send the car. While they were standing outside waiting Pradeep kept grinning and refusing to tell them what was funny. Arun jokingly threatened him and grabbed his arm.

"O.k., it's just that I want to see the expression on your face when the car arrives, and you see the driver." Arun let go of his arm and Pradeep stepped away to the side. "But I'm not telling you another thing."

A few minutes later a Rolls-Royce car pulled up and a uniformed driver got out. The uniform was something out of a movie. Pradeep nodded to them and they walked with looks of amazement to the car. The driver took their luggage and insisted on opening the doors for them.

None of them had said a word.

"It was my grandfather's, he was a minister to the last Nawab and this was a gift for his negotiating the defeat of a land reform bill just before Independence."

He made a face and they grinned and laughed with him.

The house was in the old Cantonment army quarters. It was huge and filled with old furniture. The servants fussed incredibly when they arrived. After much argument Pradeep got his grandmother to agree that for them it was much more fun to catch buses than to be chauffeur-driven. She then had an elderly scribe prepare a list of buses, routes and numbers, and places to see.

"I insist that you tell us when you want to go to Golconda Fort because we will go with you. Not in the bus of course." As she said this she looked at them all carefully, and then smiled. "Not that my sister and I will climb the hill. We will just sit and watch you lot puff up and down the steps and stairs."

The first morning they wandered around the city and saw a newly released movie that everyone was raving about at school. Neither John and Pradeep had been allowed to see it in Chintana because of studies. Arun had seen it and said it was first class. He couldn't tell them that his opinion was based on the fact that the hero's brother in the film was just the guy Arun liked to think about when he was handpumping.

In the afternoon they went to the Salan Jung Museum and walked until closing time. They were all tired and mentally exhausted at looking at all the exhibits. They would go again though, they all decided.

The next day at dawn they went to Golconda. With Pradeep's gran and aunt it was more like an expedition. Two servants went along, and when they arrived, quickly put up three umbrellas on the small grass patch just outside the massive fort gates. The boys walked and climbed and marveled at it all for hours. They got back to the main gate at lunchtime. Within minutes the servants had two card tables up and a lunch spread out. Pradeep's great-aunt told them stories about the Fort. She was a retired history teacher from Osmania University. Pradeep and John went back inside the Fort after lunch, but Arun went for three rides on a camel that was there for the tourists. The following day in the morning they went back to the Museum. They came back past the cinema and and got tickets for the evening show. They walked around the city again until five. They ate tiffin and John suggested they go back to the side streets by the cinema and wander through the sports shop. They had looked in its window in the morning. They agreed.

They entered the shop. Pradeep headed for the cricket section and John and Arun towards the hockey display. They stood a few feet from the display and looked at each other. Mr. D'Souza the Sports Master — their own S.M. — was standing there examining hockey pads.

"Good afternoon, sir," they said together like a pair of parrots. S.M. looked up, surprised to see them. Pradeep heard them laughing and came over to greet S.M.

"What are you doing sir, not buying hockey junk are you sir?" They laughed at him and his cricket bias.

A shop assistant came over. "Bring twelve of this brand in standard and junior sizes," he said before turning to the boys. "The College is buying a complete set of sports gear for cricket, hockey and badminton. Problem has been the badminton shuttles. Took me three days to find them. How long are you boys here?"

"Going home tomorrow night sir, and you?" Pradeep spoke.

"Off to Goa tomorrow if I've finished. I'd go on tonight's express if I could get someone to take the new badminton racquets and shuttles back. I can't risk packing them and sending by the lorry service."

John volunteered. "We can take them sir, we don't have much luggage. You might say we ate it all."

They laughed and explained about the food they had come with and there not being a siege in Hyderabad. He laughed with them.

"Arun has promised not to take the camel home this time too."

John added.

"I will be finished here in half an hour, like me to buy you tiffin? I can give you the racquets and shuttles too and that would allow me to get tonight's train. I really want to get home quickly."

They looked at each other. They had tickets to the first show. Arun explained the situation and watched S.M.'s face fall flat. He volunteered to go with him to pick up the stuff. He had seen the film anyway. S.M. said it wasn't necessary and that he would go tomorrow. Arun said it wasn't a problem. It wasn't either. S.M. insisted on buying them a drink of sugar-cane juice. John and Pradeep went off and Arun followed S.M. back to the sports shop.

"I didn't think the College had so much money for sports gear. You told us that even new hockey balls were a problem last month," Arun said by way of casual conversation.

Mr. D'Souza didn't look at Arun but said in a slow way, "Well what I said was true then, the College doesn't have money but a donor gave the money."

Instantly Arun knew it was his father. Three weeks ago he had asked Arun what a hockey stick cost and what pads cost. He had also said at supper one night that it was about time the girls were learning to play badminton. He thought it a strange thing for his father to say. Now it added up.

"I suppose I can guess sir, I suppose in some ways I should help and take the badminton things back, shouldn't I?"

Mr. D'Souza grinned and then patted him on the shoulder. "I said nothing Arun, that's your idea."

They took an auto-rickshaw down to Nampally where S.M. was staying in a small lodge. It overlooked the busy junction and the crowds coming and going to the station.

On the way to the lodge Arun had decided that if S.M. said anything or made any comment he would give a straight reply. Arun thought that S.M. was quite a hunky man. Sitting so close to him in the auto, their thighs rubbing as the auto bumped along the potholed street, Arun began to feel 'hot' as Krishna called it.

On the way up the stairs S.M. asked. "How's Krishna, he didn't come with you?"

Arun said lightly as he opened the door, "No, but he is well and active."

They drank water and S.M. wrapped the racquets and shuttles into a tight parcel and made a string handle.

"And you are active too, are you?"

106

Arun was standing at the window looking at the crowds go by and the way the double-decker buses swayed over at an angle as they turned the corner. He was already hard.

"Yes, Krishna was my guru."

S.M. came over and stood next to Arun. He put his hand on Arun's back and ran it down to his buttocks.

"So I can't teach you anything?"

Arun stood straighter and turned slightly,

"Only experience." Arun couldn't believe he had said that. S.M. was grinning and drew his hand from Arun's buttocks to the front of his pants and stroked his hard cock. Arun felt the zip go down. He didn't know whether to touch S.M. or not. He wanted to.

S.M. took his hand and placed it on his pants fly. He was as hard as Arun. Arun felt it and squeezed it. It was big. They stepped away from the window. S.M. walked to the door, slid the bolt up and hung a towel over the keyhole. Arun started to take his shirt off. S.M. came back and hugged him, slipped his hand to the front and unbuckled the pants belt. Arun felt his pants and underpants being drawn down. Arun had one hand inside S.M.'s shirt, the other inside his now open fly. They undressed each other. Arun groaned with delight when he held S.M.'s cock. The skin came right back and the head was bigger than he could ever have imagined. It was just as Krishna had described it...

S.M. made him sit on the bed, knelt down in front of him, took hold of Arun's pulsating cock and sucked it. Arun groaned again. S.M. lifted Arun's legs onto the bed. They sat facing each other holding each other's cocks and handpumping. S.M. gently lay Arun on his back and gave him an incredible hand job with a few sucks in between. Arun was beyond himself. He felt it surging and then it blew and he shivered with joy. He lay there for a minute and S.M. rubbed the come over his stomach. Arun sat up and with both hands pushed S.M. down to the bed and did the same to him. It took S.M. ages to come and Arun enjoyed watching him getting excited. Every time Arun massaged his balls he groaned a little. Then without warning it erupted and landed in two big shots onto S.M.'s hairy chest.

He just lay there. When he sat up he said, "Krishna is a good teaching person."

Arun laughed. "Maybe because of *his* teacher."

S.M. grabbed him and they hugged. "Let's take a shower together."

In the shower they were both still hard and did it all again. Arun's legs felt weak.

"You really are sexy aren't you?" S.M. said smiling at Arun.

"Yes, I am. You make me feel that way too."

Arun arrived back to Pradeep's grandmother's before Pradeep and John and explained what had happened. Well, not everything! She plied him with hot samosa tiffin followed by a cardamom-flavored milk sweet and a large cup of brewed coffee. She sent the servant out to the front verandah with a cane chair for him and had the servant put the radio on the window shelf.

"My sister and I are going over the road to our friend's house. Tell Pradeep to call me when he comes home."

The two women walked with sticks across the road, carrying a torch. Pradeep and John came home and said that Arun looked like a grandfather sitting in the cane chair and listening to the radio. He explained what Gran had said.

They sat around and commented on the film. John looked at Arun closely: "You look very happy for someone who missed the cinema."

"Yes, he and S.M. went down to Nampally and visited the red-light houses there and had a fuck each."

John laughed and ran his hand up Arun's legs and pinched his thigh. "True or not?" he asked.

"True," Arun said to make John stop pinching.

Pradeep went over to get his gran and aunt.

The visit to Hyderabad was a fascinating experience for all of them. Arun had his two extra secret experiences. One he had labeled in his mind as 'The Punjabi Adventure' — a story he would certainly want to share with Krishna guru, after sharing the 'S.M. Experience' story as well!

Gran insisted on going to the Secunderabad Railway Station with them. "After all you have all that extra sports equipment to take, and you have to take at least one basket of food with you for the trip."

The night before they were to leave Pradeep's uncle had come to visit. He had been in the States for six months and only recently returned. He had not seen Pradeep since his return. He had opened an electronics shop in the new Taj Towers complex in Hyderabad. He gave Pradeep a small case with gifts for his family. Pradeep wanted to know what the gifts were, but his uncle just laughed and told him he would have to wait until his father opened it.

Arun asked him about the exchange rate between the American dollar and the Indian rupee. He patiently explained it all, and took out a new model calculator to explain it. Arun had never seen one like that before and asked him how to do square roots on it. He knew his father would be fascinated with something that made calculations so easy.

Pradeep's father and sister were at the station to meet them. Arun was sorry that Krishna was in his native village for the night when he reached home. His sisters asked a lot of questions and Chitti wanted to know strange things about what he saw and didn't see in Hyderabad! He waited until supper and then gave them a present each. They were delighted. Chitti immediately set up the new game on the table for them to play.

"I purchased something for you too Dad. It cost a lot, and I have to send the money to Pradeep's gran but she said it's alright. Her son came one evening. I told him you were a contractor. He showed me this." Arun pulled out the pocket calculator. "You can do timber and other calculations really quick on it."

The others played their game and Arun showed his father how the calculator worked. They sat with it for two hours. His father was excited beyond words.

The holidays passed and three days before the new term Arun's father called him. "You know the S.M. at College, take this envelope to him. Be careful, it has some money I owe him."

Arun rode his bicycle down to the College and saw the light on in S.M.'s room. The grounds were empty. The sun had just gone down. Storm clouds were in the sky puffing themselves up and rolling over fiercely.

Arun knocked. S.M. called out, "Come in." He was taking his shirt off, Arun presumed, to take a bath.

"My father sent this envelope for you. It has money in it."

Arun put it on the table and found a bronze paperweight to put on it. He could hardly stop himself from laughing out aloud. It was a casting of a Nandi bull. He wondered if Krishna had noticed it!

"Want to take a bath too?" S.M. asked casually, but Arun saw the bulge in his shorts.

Arun turned and locked the door. They took each other's clothing off in the bathroom. S.M. poured hot water into the cement tank. They sat on the floor with legs entwined and poured water slowly over each other. S.M. had coconut oil rubbed in his hair. Arun reached up and took the container off the stool. He poured some onto S.M.'s pubics and over his cock.

S.M. held his hand out and Arun poured some oil into it. Arun felt the change of sensation and shivered with joy. They drew close to each other. Slowly S.M. raised Arun onto his legs. Arun saw him put more oil on his hand. He slipped it under Arun's balls and slowly massaged it into Arun's hole. The feeling was beyond description. Arun pulled himself closer and felt both pain and joy as S.M. gently pressed his cock inside. Arun clung to S.M. He wrapped his arms around his shoulders. He didn't remember much of the details, just the new feeling that was rippling through him in waves of pain and pleasure.

S.M. shuddered and Arun felt the pulsation inside him as his cock convulsed and the semen shot out. Then Arun sat upright as he himself surged and felt his own cream rush out. He looked down and saw it all over S.M.'s hairy chest.

They bathed.

Arun saw S.M. on the recreation ground. They were always together during hockey training. They said nothing special to each other and acted as though nothing had happened. At the end of one late afternoon training session S.M. took Arun's hockey stick. "This handle needs tape. Bring it to me later."

Arun was caught. He couldn't leave the house that night, because John was coming to study some extra physics.

"Sir, can I bring it tomorrow night."

"Sure."

The next night Arun took his hockey stick for taping. Thus it began. More than eight years of friendship. Eight years of two and three times a week. Eight years of meeting in all kinds of places at all hours of the night and sometimes day. Getting to Hyderabad three times and Madras twice. Four times on sports trips to other schools they managed to stay together. It was made easier when Arun became junior and then senior hockey captain. No one ever said anything. Both were outwardly as straight as anyone else. They just happened to be two guys, one young, one older — and both liked — well both were men who loved men.

Krishna thought it was fantastic. He joined them a few times but he seemed more interested in just having it with Arun. Arun told him about the way S.M. had penetrated him. Krishna wanted to know all of the details, from how he did it to how it felt.

"Arun, if you only knew. I have wanted to do that to you ever since the first time. I really wanted to. I just didn't know if I could. I was frightened you would think it wrong or something."

Arun would look at all the guys in the class, or the guys playing hockey. Was he the only one? Were he and Krishna and S.M. the only ones? Maybe they were. Guys made comments about handpumping and things like that, but it never seemed to go beyond words. John and Pradeep never said or asked anything. Maybe he was in a minority.

Arun smiled. "Great minority feeling," he said quietly to himself looking in the mirror.

III. Shiva's Wedding

The Invitation

ARUN'S FATHER had them all seated on the front verandah. The electricity had been going on and off all day, the house was hot and the air was humid.

It was Sunday afternoon. They all wanted to go to the cinema, but he was being difficult, as he often seemed to be of late. They were interested to go to the cinema for many reasons. One simply being that the cinema had its own generator and was air conditioned, another that the film was supposed to be rather daring.

"At Rotary last week the School Inspector said that Indian students' knowledge of geography is a disgrace. Some students don't even know their state capitals."

The two girls made quick glances at their younger brother, they were having a bet on how many times 'Rotary' would be used in one week. Every time he wanted to make some point, or to impress them that what he said was correct, Rotary somehow became the authority. Then he put down the rules for going to the cinema.

Arun was to keep the scores and with an atlas his father asked them all questions. To go to the cinema each must get sixty per cent and the total of them averaged must be at least seventy. They argued for merit points but he just laughed. Their mother sat in her large cane chair and pretended to be asleep.

The gate latch creaked and they all looked up. Arun could tell by his father's face that he was very surprised.

"Well, Venkatramu's son-in-law, come in, come in. Sit down."

The man ignored the invitation to sit. He smiled and handed Mr. Muddli an envelope painted bright turmeric yellow.

Arun watched his father place the invitation on the table. He casually picked it up. It must have taken them hours to dab each corner with the turmeric paste. Arun shook his head slightly. These were the kind of rituals that wasted hours of time for nothing. In his opinion at least such rituals were a waste of time. He also now realized that there were a lot of rituals and demanding family customs that were an imposition. Like having your parents select who you were to marry. Worse still, absolutely no option as to whether you even wanted to get married.

"All of your family are invited to attend the marriage feast." He paused. "Venkatramu asked if you will be starting the platform tomorrow afternoon as agreed."

Ramesh Muddli nodded, "Of course I will, but..." he paused this time.

"Oh yes, Venkatramu said that he would send you the payment tomorrow, and to tell you that the timber was also to be delivered tomorrow morning."

Ramesh smiled and nodded and the man left without a smile, closing the gate with a slight bang.

No one spoke. They knew they didn't have to. Their father would definitely make a comment. He had been making comments for the last two weeks on the job he was doing.

Venkatramu the pujari at the big temple had arranged for Shiva his youngest son's marriage. The Brahmin carpenter who usually did all of their work refused because of some major argument concerning the bride's parents. Most who knew the families believed it was more likely that he wouldn't do the work because of payment problems. Venkatramu was known for his meanness and his arguments over the final payment.

Ramesh Muddli was accustomed to dealing with such people. When he had received a message to call and see Venkatramu he had ignored the first request, and the second and the third. Finally Venkatramu came himself to the house Ramesh was contract building.

"I'll do it by contract only. You buy the materials I tell you, and pay me twenty per cent in advance on each unit of the contract."

Venkatramu was shocked, or acted so when he was told this. The house walls on one side all had to be plastered. The aprons around the wells had to be resealed. New steps were needed at two doors. The kitchen needed the fireplace rebuilt. At the temple one wall gate needed a new brick pillar, and two windows had to be replaced in the long guest room.

Mr. Muddli was so happy with the invitation that they were allowed to stop the geography test. "I won't eat the day before just so I get my money's worth at the dinner."

The children laughed.

On Monday morning Arun asked John, "Venkatramu from the temple is having his youngest son married next week. Are you going to the dinner?"

John nodded and jumped on the back of the motorbike. As they went across the railway crossing John said, "Shiva and Sam are close friends. Shiva came himself yesterday and gave us all an invitation. He doesn't sound very happy about it. It's typically all been arranged without his opinion."

Fears of Marriage

SHIVA WASN'T happy in any way about the whole marriage thing. It had been forced on him. He was filled with doubts and fears of many things, and one in particular.

His fears were such that he couldn't share with anyone. He couldn't, or wouldn't, or was even maybe frightened to discuss it with Sam, who was his best friend. He couldn't bring himself to even ask Ramu about it. He could hear what Ramu would say: 'Don't worry, once you get married it will work.' Ramu had got married a year ago. It had been a sudden family arrangement, just like this, and Ramu hadn't said anything for or against it. He just accepted it. In the last year Ramu had been able to come only once in two months. He always stayed three nights and Shiva felt no real change in his interest and desire. Ramu talked a lot about his wife and their family problems, which rather bored Shiva. But he certainly hadn't lost interest if it was a weekend visit and Ab was there. The 'trio' turned Ramu on more than Shiva had ever imagined possible.

What no one knew was the truth about Shiva and Sam's visit to the prostitutes' house. It seemed long ago now but the memory of it was so vivid in Shiva's mind that it was always just like yesterday. Sam and Shiva had gone together that first time. Shiva had begged Sam to go in with him. In the end Sam even agreed that by paying the woman a little extra they would both have it with her together. Shiva begged Sam to do it first so he could watch. Sam thought it was crazy but agreed. It wasn't the woman on the bed with her saree pulled up that turned Shiva on, but Sam with his pants off and his hard cock. Shiva had never seen Sam hard. It was thick and really curved. Sam made neat grunting sounds.

He stopped halfway through the job. "Now you start, but don't blow, stop like I did and pull out, and then go in again after me."

Shiva did what Sam told him.

He thought afterwards, not once but so many times, that it

115

was interesting. But it was Sam being there with his hard cock that made it so. It had so worried Shiva for months that he decided to try again, but without Sam. Without even telling Sam.

It took months to pluck up courage. He didn't dare go to the same woman, or even the same house. He went to another house he had heard the students talking about near the Railway Station over-head bridge. He was frightened that if he went to the same house the woman might tell Sam.

At first it went alright. He got a hard simply because he was thinking of the first time. Thinking of Sam's big curved cock. He went in and then it started to go soft. He concentrated his mind but it didn't help.

The woman asked what was wrong. He said that he hadn't been well. She said that it sometimes happened. She even suggested that he eat some mutton. It would make him strong.

On the way home he laughed. He could imagine telling his devout mother to buy and cook him some meat because a prostitute said it would make his cock hard.

Deep inside him though he wasn't laughing. He knew the truth. He would fuck Abdullah every Friday he came. If he was home Friday and Saturday he would do it both nights with Abdullah. It was having Abdullah's cock in one hand and screwing him at the same time. It was looking at Abdullah's body that turned him on. It was Abdullah's teasing of his cock. It was Abdullah's way of slowly drawing closer until Shiva couldn't resist Abdullah's invitation to 'go in'.

It was Ab. It was a man. The feeling grew stronger than any-thing else. The feeling that he, Shiva, was a person, a man, *a man who loved men.*

He understood that his relationship with Ramu was basically, by Ramu's decision, just sex. With Abdullah it was different. They were both physically and emotionally really attracted to each other. They did little intimate things.

Many times Shiva said it straight out, "Ab I love you."

Abdullah would smile and whisper back, "I love you more, too."

Shiva knew that he didn't hate women. In fact there were a lot of young women that he enjoyed talking to. He thought that some of them were really pretty. He agreed with Sam many times when he said, 'Now she's a beauty isn't she?' Shiva would look and usu-ally agree.

Once they had nearly had an accident on the bicycle because of Sam's 'tits-watching', as he called it. They were going around the Clock Tower corner, where there was a policeman on point duty directing traffic. Sam was riding and Shiva sitting on the bar.

"That's her, the one with the blue sari. She is the prettiest girl in the arts class. Wish she would model for us. Breasts like hard, large, and very firm lemons."

Shiva said to Sam quietly, "Is that her brother with her?"

"Yes." Sam replied.

"I'd sooner fuck him then."

And that's when Sam nearly overbalanced and hit the policeman, who stuck out his foot to push the bicycle away and shouted at them.

Shiva had another memory that always came to him. The next year Sam had done the same birthday trick. But this time he had said that they wouldn't be doing it together. He didn't like the idea of being watched. Shiva laughed. They went to the first-show cinema and on the way to the house Sam got them a sample-size bottle of brandy each. It was the first time Shiva had drunk it. It burnt like unimaginable fire in his throat and stomach. They got to the house and Sam chattered to the three girls. He organized the whole thing without Shiva saying a thing. They walked down the passage and into a small room. Shiva heard Sam next door.

It worked, but it worked for only one reason, Shiva knew that. It worked because he imagined what Sam was doing. Shiva imagined that he was with Sam, like the first time. He got hard and lay with the woman. She smiled and gently brushed his hair. He played with her breasts, because she put his hand on them. He went in, and then it happened again — it went down, it lost its heat, its interest. He concentrated, but nothing. It was as though his cock had vanished from his mind. Then he closed his eyes and imagined Ab. It came hard again for a minute or so and then flat again. He withdrew and made a long groaning noise. A few seconds later Shiva heard Sam make his 'final' grunt.

They laughed about how great it was on the way home. Shiva couldn't tell him the truth.

When Ramu got married Shiva said to Abdullah, "What are you going to do when your family tells you that they have arranged your marriage?"

Ab looked at him. They were sitting on the bed. It was late and dark in the room. A sliver of light came in from the window from the full moon outside. The light fell across Shiva's face. Ab leaned closer.

"When I finish this degree I can get a job anywhere." He paused and leaned across and took Shiva's hand. "My grandfather left me a small house in Hyderabad. People are renting it now."

He paused and Shiva saw that Abs had a very sad but determined look on his face. His voice sounded stern. Shiva knew the tone — it was Abs' 'final word' tone.

"If they..." he paused and shook his head slightly. "Well of course the truth is, if my father puts too much pressure on me I'm telling them the truth. I'm not getting married."

He looked at Shiva and smiled. "I can get a job in Hyderabad and live in the house. It's mine. They can't touch the property. It was put in my name when I was circumcised. My grandfather is dead now, I have every right to it. They will argue and shout and try to force me by using all kinds of words and excuses. They will even threaten to cut me off from the community. I don't care. I know that."

He stopped. He took his hand away from Shiva and sat quietly for a minute, Shiva said nothing. Abs just sat playing with the buttons on his shirt.

"Go on" Shiva said quietly.

"Well I know that I'm a *man that simply loves men...*" he lifted his leg onto the bed, and took Shiva's hand again. He was looking directly at Shiva's face. "Maybe I should say, I'm a man that loves you. I do love you Shiva. My dream is that you might one day come and live in Hyderabad too. You could get a job."

"I agree, it's possible. Why not? I know what you say. It's the same feeling I have."

Tonight though the words came back to Shiva bitterly. He had meant them, but all of a sudden he was caught up with his family. He didn't have a chance to say anything. It wasn't a question. It was just all settled without him. It was so far advanced by the time he was told that he couldn't speak. He knew he was wrong not to speak up. He knew that somehow he had been wrong to remain silent. He knew he had somehow betrayed Ab too.

Ab said nothing though when he told him about the marriage arrangement. Just smiled, shook his head a little.

Shiva even felt that his whole college education had been a waste too. All he had to do now was sit in his proposed father-in-law's shop and count money all day.

The days to the marriage grew shorter and shorter. The house became more and more like a circus. He just walked around doing nothing.

The marriage was fixed for Thursday morning at 2.17 a.m. What a stupid typical Brahmin time! How could anyone believe that 2.17 in the morning was an auspicious time for a marriage! How could anyone in their right mind say it was the correct time! Whatever Shiva heard about the marriage made him feel less and less interested. He smiled outwardly to everyone though.

Shanti caught him a few times looking dejected. She asked what was wrong. He just said that he was tired with all of the things going on. She smiled at him, but he knew she didn't believe him.

Then the day came. By eleven in the morning he was tired. He and the bride sat like stuffed peacock and peahen on decorated cushions. People moved like ants in all directions. The marquee tent was huge. It had been erected in front of the house, and completely blocked the road for the day. A few people complained, but no one dared say anything too much.

The police of course said nothing. The sub-inspector was the uncle of the bride. The smell of incense and smoke from the ritual fire Shiva and his bride had walked around seven times filled the tent. The smell of food was overpowering but he couldn't eat until evening. It was a hot day too.

He had a headache. He had looked at his wife but she sat head down with her sari pulled tightly over her head, as was the custom. Presents and gifts piled up on a table.

At eleven-thirty the only cheerful thing of the morning happened: Sam laughed. Sam's whole family, except their father who didn't come, sat as close as possible to him while they ate.

As they left Sam came up and slipped a small card into his hand and winked at him. Sam turned and said, "Happy Birthday."

Sam's mother looked round. "What a stupid thing to say on a person's marriage day. You are totally brainless sometimes Samuel."

Sam shrugged his shoulders and waved back to Shiva.

On the way out of the tent John saw Arun and his family eating on the other side. He waved and made a sign to Arun to see him later outside. Sweets were being served outside under a separate coconut-leaf tent.

"Waited for you," John said. He looked around. "Caught a glance of the bride. She looks really pretty."

Arun nodded and smiled. He hadn't seen the bride's face at all. He had seen the bridegroom though. Sitting in a white lunghi, stomach and chest bare, covered in oil. Arun couldn't tell John what he thought.

IV. Arun's Decision

College Reunion

MANY OF the ex-students had sent their acceptance letters to the College out of some sense of duty that they couldn't define. Several included cheques and money orders for the fund towards the new hall because they knew they wouldn't really make it to the function.

Others were excited at the idea of seeing fellow students after so many years of going their different ways.

The person most excited about the idea was Arun's father, simply because he would be the contractor for the new hall. It was to be big and it was prestigious to have the contract to build it. Arun went along with his excitement. It was hard not to. He also tried not to argue because he knew that his father was still a little upset with him. He knew that his decision to do a B.Ed. after his B.Sc. was both a point of pride and a point of contention with his father. He really wanted Arun to be part of the building and contract business he had established, more involved in the day-to-day management. Arun still did some monthly checking with the accountant who worked full-time for his father now, but that wasn't what his father really wanted. On the other hand he was proud that Arun not only graduated with honours but also got an appointment to teach in the College. His gift of appreciation to the College had been a huge addition of books and equipment to the Science Lab.

Chitti, Arun's younger brother, seemed to have no option but to join his father. Chitti already had Arun's old motorbike from the day Arun got the new Rajdoot for getting his degree. Arun had even joined Rotaract — the junior Rotary Club — to keep peace with his family. It wasn't such a bad club, though he found the business conversation a bit thick at times.

Three days before the reunion Abdullah took an auto-rickshaw out to Corot Industries and found Sam in his office. He was plant supervisor and had a glass-partitioned office overlooking the factory floor.

"Abdullah, long time no see, friend." Sam stood up and shook

Abdullah's hand.

"Well I don't come this side much now. I'm in Hyderabad mostly. When I'm not in New Delhi that is — fighting with the government babus." He smiled and took the seat Sam offered.

"What are you doing?"

Abdullah felt it was a genuine question and not the usual polite chatter of friends that have drifted apart.

"Well I'm a good Muslim," Abdullah laughed. "I started a small leather goods unit almost in a cupboard and it grew into a small factory."

"And now you have your wife locked up in the cupboard I suppose." Sam liked his own joke and laughed. Abdullah laughed louder though.

"No Sam I'm still single and have absolutely no plans to change that." A quick thought ran through Abdullah's mind that maybe Sam hadn't heard of the big family argument over him refusing to marry his cousin.

"Well I suppose I should have kept my wife locked up in the cupboard more often. I've got three kids now. One after the other."

"I came to ask if you were going to the reunion thing. I am half planning to go, but I wanted to go with someone. I'm not sure who is here nowadays and I didn't want to go if none of us were there."

Sam sat quietly in his chair, his expression changed. "Well I had almost decided not to go. My brother John keeps asking me though." He paused and looked up to the ceiling. "I suppose I was feeling a bit like you." He looked quickly down and smiled at Abdullah, "Yes, come on, we'll go. I'm sure that Sreenu and a few of the others will turn up late as always."

He turned his face away from Abdullah and looked back at the ceiling. He was tapping a pencil on the table. Without any expression in his voice he said quietly, without looking away from the ceiling. "You know —" he paused again, "well I suppose I didn't want to really go... without Shiva."

The door opened and a peon came in with tea.

"Good, that's settled, we'll go. You come around to my place any time Sunday, we'll spend the day together too."

They chatted and drank tea. Abdullah felt better by the time he left and made his way home, where he felt rather isolated from the family by their silence. On the rare times that Abdullah went home, and his father was in the room or close by, no one spoke.

Early in the evening he was sitting on the roof verandah looking down on the narrow street. Two young men came riding along slowly on a motorbike and then stopped at the house. They stood there talking to someone. A few minutes later his younger brother came up the stairs — the only one brave enough always speak to him as though there was no ban against Abdullah being treated humanely in his family's house.

From the day he had left, he always found it hard to come home. It was the silence that got to him. He wouldn't ever come if it wasn't for his aged mother.

She understood nothing of the whole affair, she said. Her constant comment when anyone spoke to her was, "Not women's business."

His brother Shar called from the rooftop door, "Two guys want to see you, one's the brother of your friend Sam."

Abdullah hurried down the stairs.

"Abdullah I'm John, Sam's younger brother, remember me?" This is my friend Arun."

Abdullah smiled and nodded to them both.

"Well Sam said that there is an old boys' cricket match against the present College team on Friday. He is taking the day off, if you are willing to play. He wants to play I think."

Abdullah grinned.

John grinned back. "Yes, he is a bit fat for it now, still the exercise will be good for him."

Abdullah laughed with them. "Are you two playing?"

They laughed at him. "Cricket, you are joking, we are into the real thing — hockey, man."

Abdullah took a joking swipe at them and they jumped back and turned to the motorbike.

"Sam said come around for breakfast at eight in the morning. It starts sharp at nine."

Arun revved the bike up and they went down the street tooting. They waved back to him at the corner.

Abdullah looked at his watch. He went inside and washed, dressed in his old white 'uniform' and walked to the mosque. He still went to prayers when he had time. He knew that it threw his father into a tither of great confusion because he couldn't cope with the thought of *a man who loved men* being a true Muslim.

He had tried to tell his father about famous Muslim leaders and rulers who had both male and female love affairs. It was a waste of time. He often thought that his problem must be like a Brahmin gay telling his father that the *Karma Sutra* and the wall engravings at Puri Temple were real. He smiled to himself.

The next day's cricket match was a disaster for the old boys. They got properly beaten. They all admitted to S.M. that it was due to lack of exercise and too much fat. S.M. who was still as fit as ever agreed with them. The old boys' hockey team suffered the same fate.

The cricket match ended early and they all wandered over to see the final of the hockey. Abdullah saw that Arun, who he had met the day before, was umpire. He really was tall. Abdullah watched more of the umpiring than the actual game.

It was a long time since he had felt so attracted to anyone. It wasn't as though he didn't have a sex life in Hyderabad. He did, but it was all mostly one-night stands, quickies that served one purpose and did little else really. He knew that. Maybe one day he would be in the right frame of mind again to look for a real love life.

He knew that he wanted someone like Shiva again. He needed a regular relationship. Every time he thought about it though he thought of old experiences, old disappointments.

On Sunday they all met at Sam's house. Sreenu didn't arrive until half an hour before the function. John had left early and got seats organized in the front for them to sit together. It was long and quite interesting, both serious and comical with the skits put on. Sam got the 'Most Productive Old Boy's Award' and made a totally comic speech that made even the fathers laugh.

When Abdullah had the chance, he turned to Arun. "Here's my card. If you ever come to Hyderabad, call me. I've plenty of room if you want to stay."

Arun felt the warmth of the words, and smiled.

Later Arun lay on his bed, the fan turned up to speed three. It was humid and he felt sticky. He was half dreaming about the day. It had been great really. He was thinking about a bath. Thinking about that made him think of Krishna. He hadn't seen him for months. It was harvesting season and he would be busy on his wife's family land. He had to agree with Krishna that the marriage his father had arranged for him was really a great chance in life. Arun's father had been in Krishna's village building a small temple. One thing led to another and he agreed to build Krishna a small two-roomed house with a tile roof as part of the marriage contract for a girl who would have three acres of land given to her by her mother.

The girl had been a little wild in her early years and some of her family were against the marriage. Krishna had nothing to offer. His father was dead and his mother was aged. His only sister was married and now lived in Madras. Krishna's mother had only a small plot of dry waste land and a hutment. Krishna knew about the girl's history but he didn't care. In his own way he too had been wild in his younger days. He knew that Arun would miss him. Arun did miss him too. Not that Arun was without 'satisfying company'. It was strange really. Arun had finished up being a real lover to Krishna's own 'guru' — S.M.

Arun had spent a few minutes late on the reunion talking to S.M. They agreed to meet on Tuesday night. He took a bath and got hard, thinking not about S.M. or Krishna, but about Abdullah. He had given him a card. Arun looked at it before he stripped to bathe. He had almost felt a vibration pass between them as he took the card. He was going to Hyderabad in a month's time. He had arranged to go to the University and get information on the change of textbooks that had been half announced.

Other than Krishna and then S.M., Arun had not ventured into any other relationship, not even a 'quickie' — though he could have, he was sure, with several guys. There was a new teacher on the Hindi staff, a one-year relief, who had made oblique suggestions several times. Arun was tempted, but he didn't want to upset S.M.. He had never mentioned it to S.M.. He somehow felt that S.M. wouldn't like it.

He dried himself and got dressed. He felt restless. He walked through the house. They were all watching tv.

He walked to the gate and heard the P.A. system blaring from a marriage tent in the next street. He would go for a ride into town on the Rajdoot, maybe he would see someone interesting to talk to. The only problem was that whenever he did that he usually ran into Ashok or Dinesh or Shastri from the Rotaract and they would talk for hours about inconsequential things. Pet projects designed to give Rotaract publicity and one or two particular Rotarians a large dose of limelight.

He cruised along slowly and nearly hit a guy who jumped right out in front of him. He braked suddenly and was about to shout when he realized in the light that it was John.

"You really scared me. I thought it must have been some guy that was boozed or cracked."

John came around to the side of the Rajdoot and laughed. "Truth is that I am a little boozed. Sam and I and Dinish got a bottle of brandy to celebrate today's great reunion and all that." He wasn't too straight on his legs and held on to Arun's shoulder. "Come on take me home. I shouldn't be out like this."

As they turned down the lane John nearly fell off the motor-bike and his mother shouted like Arun had never heard her before. Then Arun saw Dinesh and Abdullah trying to lift the cot with Sam on it inside. He was asleep on it fully boozed. With Sam safely inside and his wife obviously angry and John apologizing every couple of minutes, their mother produced coffee. "I thought you lot were bad enough when you were students, you are worse now you are ex-students," she said with a smile. "Thank goodness this reunion doesn't happen every year."

She turned to Arun. "Can you please take a letter to the night shift supervisor at Corot. Tell them Sam isn't well." She paused and laughed, "Which is true I suppose. Too much so."

She sighed, shook her head and went inside. She came out a few minutes later with more coffee and a note. "Abdullah, will you go with you Arun, it's quite a way if the rail gate is closed and it's dark on that road."

Abdullah looked at Arun. "Sure, I can get down at the junction on the way back."

The road to Corot was still under repair. There were two detours, with more potholes than road. For almost a kilometre it was totally corrugated. The motorbike chugged along slowly. Abdullah held onto Arun, both hands firmly on Arun's arms. Arun could feel himself becoming aroused. Arun was sure he was imagining it, but he thought he could feel a hard cock press against him every so often as the bike slowed or swerved around potholes. The factory gate was closed and a Nepalese night watchman came out of his guard hut. He spoke to them and looked at the note and opened the gate. He recorded the bike numberplate. Arun stopped the bike in the parking area. Abdullah slipped off and Arun pulled the bike back onto its stand. He pulled the key out and turned around to Abdullah. He couldn't miss Abdullah adjusting his cock in his pants. They smiled at each other.

As they walked to the main gate, Arun said, almost without thinking, "Sometimes riding pillion on the bike makes you horny, I think it's the vibration." Abdullah laughed and simply said, "Yes, maybe it's that."

The shift supervisor took the note, read it and said, "Thanks." They turned and walked out. He wasn't happy about Sam not coming in, that was obvious.

Arun started the bike and as Abdullah sat behind him he said quietly as a question, "Does riding over bumps and the vibration make you horny sometimes too?"

Arun realized that his answer was 'uninviting' but it was too late after the words came out. "Used to but I've got used to it now."

They were at the gate and the watchman waved them out.

"Bad luck." Abdullah said.

Arun pretended he didn't hear properly. "Bad luck what?" He turned his head slightly as he asked, a wind had started to blow.

"Bad luck that you don't get a horn riding anymore. I could have held onto it as we went over those bumps and I wouldn't be so likely to fall off."

He laughed a little and nudged Arun with his elbow.

The roadside Punjabi hotel was still open as they came to the ring-road turn. Arun turned in. "You order egg and roti for me, and I'll pull over to the petrol bunk and fill up."

"Great idea."

Abdullah slipped off. Arun rode to the bunk. He fuelled up, pulled the bike to one side and walked back to the hotel. Abdullah was sitting on a cot like the Punjabi lorry drivers do. Arun sat opposite him.

A tall young Punjabi guy came over with their order. Arun took the plate slowly from him. The guy was really handsome. He watched Abdullah and smiled to himself. Abdullah seemed to be taking even more time to take the plate. He pulled a handkerchief from his pocket and took a minute to flick it open and lay it on his lap.

"Some Punjabis are really handsome aren't they?" Arun made the comment as he broke off roti and dipped it into the chutney.

"Handsome, and sexy looking too, I think."

They looked at each other. Abdullah smiled. They ate in silence for a while and then started to chat about the reunion day. Abdullah insisted on paying.

They came to the first detour and slowed down. They were halfway round when an idiot lorry driver came across in the opposite direction. Arun edged the bike carefully to the side and said, "Hang on tight."

Then Arun had to really concentrate. His mind was in a flip. Abdullah was holding on tight and chuckling. "Like this" was all he said.

As they came out of the detour Abdullah took his hands away from Arun's crotch, but it was too late, Arun already had an erection and Abdullah had felt it clearly. Arun was feeling hotter than the exhaust pipe on his bike.

When they came to the second detour Abdullah said, "Will I hold on tight again?"

Arun didn't have to answer. It was the most exciting motorbike ride he had ever had. He had many times fantasized that something like this might happen. He often had different guys on the bike with him. He would lay awake and think about what it would have been like if they had done what Abdullah was now doing.

This was no 'on the bed' fantasy, this was reality. They were riding slowly along the road and Abdullah had unzipped his pants and had one hand inside rubbing it up and down Arun's hard cock. Arun could feel the pressure in his balls building up!

The road was divided by a safety fence as it was a lorry highway junction.

"I wish we could go somewhere. I can't invite you home, it's too complicated."

Abdullah was sitting on the bike and Arun was straddling it, the motor ticking over quietly.

"I know a place." Arun put the bike into gear. He rode home first, putting the bike into neutral for the last stretch and it silently carried them along. He stopped just short of the gate and quietly went around to his room. The house was in darkness. He could hear his father snoring. Somehow he didn't want to go into his room with Abdullah. He liked the idea of going over to the St. Thomas's hockey training field. There were two huge banyan trees there. He took the blanket and threw it over his shoulder. He slipped a small jar of cream into his pocket, and another handkerchief. He grabbed the plastic water bottle off the verandah hook.

They sat on the blanket under the tree. There was a half moon that kept hiding behind quick-moving clouds. It was silent. In the far distance only an occasional lorry could be heard. Even the dogs seemed to be quiet.

They chatted about different things for a short time. Abdullah was rubbing his hand up and down Arun's leg. Arun turned to Abdullah and they faced each other and kissed. Arun had never kissed anyone other than S.M. so passionately. Abdullah knew that he too had never kissed like this for a very long time. It had been with a friend whom he loved deeply and passionately. It was too long ago, but the memory was still vivid. Vivid and sad to think about.

"What do you like?" Abdullah asked quietly as they drew away breathing deeply.

Arun paused, tonight he would like anything and everything. "Whatever you like, I'm feeling really hot."

Abdullah laughed quietly. "Me too, must be the half moon." He stood up and took Arun's hand. They hugged and kissed again, and slowly started to undress each other.

Arun felt himself gulp as he unzipped Abdullah and slid his hand inside. He had no underpants on, and his cock was hard and big. He wrapped his hands around the head. It was like a club.

He couldn't resist it, he knelt down in front of Abdullah and pulled his pants down. Abdullah lifted his feet out. Holding his balls with one hand Arun took the hard rod fully into his mouth and felt the jolt of pleasure go through Abdullah. After a while Abdullah slipped his hands under Arun's arms and lifted him up. Then he knelt and slowly pulled Arun's underpants and pants down. Arun stepped out of them. Abdullah played with Arun's pulsating cock for ages and then with a tight mouth sucked him until he felt he would blow if Abdullah didn't stop. Abdullah sensed it and pulled away.

They lay together for a while, just stroking each other tenderly. Then Abdullah gently turned Arun on his back and knelt over him. Arun knew that people called this 'sixty-nine'. Abdullah shifted slightly and Arun took his cock into his mouth. Abdullah was overjoyed at the feeling. He was kneeling over Arun and Arun had hold of his balls and was massaging them gently and sucking him and he had this long firm cock in his mouth. It had been so long since he had met anyone who liked it like this, just like he did.

Abdullah drew away and turned and lay again next to Arun. "I've got some cream in my trousers pocket."

Abdullah reached for the pants and took the cream jar out.

"Ha, I use this too, and not just for my hair." He took the lid off, fingered some out, and rubbed it round and round Arun's cockhead until he almost screamed, and grabbed Abdullah's wrist to stop. Arun was laying on his back as Abdullah knelt across him. He used a lot of cream and guided Arun firmly into him. Arun moved his hips up slowly, and Abdullah felt him enter right in deep. Arun stretched his arms out. He held Abdullah's buttocks with one and started to stroke Abdullah's throbbing cock. Abdullah moved up and down.

Arun groaned and made three or four solid thrusts and Abdullah felt the pulsating ejaculation inside him. It was beyond imagination. As Arun relaxed Abdullah felt himself coming, and shot all over Arun's hairy chest. They lay on top of each other panting and sweating. Not speaking, why should they? Who needed words to describe what they both felt?

A train whistle blew in the distance and two dogs started to howl. Arun stopped the motorbike and Abdullah got off.

"I know there isn't a need to say anything, but, well, thanks. Come and see me any time you are in Hyderabad — I'd love to have you..."

They smiled at each other, held hands for a minute and Arun rode home feeling somehow good. He wouldn't tell S.M., well not immediately anyway.

Resignation

ON TUESDAY morning all teaching staff received a note, folded and stapled closed. Arun was in the middle of demonstrating a friction lesson with two wood blocks. He stopped to read the note, quickly finished the demonstration and gave the students a difficult problem associated with it.

He sat at his desk and reread the note. He was absolutely numb.

Emergency staff meeting — Tuesday — today —
MORNING BREAK at the Headmaster's Office.
Bell will ring ten minutes early, be prompt. All
must attend without exception or excuse. Mr. D'Souza
the Sports Master has resigned and left the College this
morning. Please do not discuss this with students or staff
until meeting time.

Arun answered a few students' questions and gave them extra notes to read and extra homework. He walked out of the room and stood on the balcony overlooking the courtyard. Over on the sports field boys were running in relays. Mr. Gupta the 'rotation' teacher was supervising them.

Arun couldn't believe it. He had seen S.M. on Friday night.

They had made slow and rather passionate love together, or Arun had made it to S.M. He had been a little quiet, but that wasn't unusual on a Friday.

Arun shook his head. Surely he had not been having sex with any of the students. But what else could it be?

No of course it wasn't anything like that. Something terrible must have happened to his family in Goa. Still if it was that, why didn't he send a message to him? Arun had said he couldn't see him on Monday because he had so many term papers to set. They had planned to meet tonight.

The bell rang. The students poured out of the classrooms like rats deserting a sinking ship. The noise level rose. They surged in all directions and Arun wove his way downstairs and along the corridor to the Head's office. It was a large room filled with cabinets of trophies and banners. Half the staff were already there. They stood and sat around but no one spoke. The Head was writing notes. He looked up and the school bursar counted everyone. He seemed confused, as always. Read the names you fool, Arun thought.

The Head was annoyed. "Read the names please."

People answered and everyone was there except Mrs. Mathu who had already marked herself as sick and gone home. The Head sat back in swivel chair.

"Over the weekend we had a senior student complain that Mr. D'Souza had made an improper remark and suggestion to him." He looked down and tapped his pencil. "Mr. D'Souza neither admitted or denied the remark or incident. I asked for his resignation last night and he has left us. I don't wish to discuss the matter further. I would appreciate the staff being discreet about it and to avoid conversations with students or the public."

He looked up.

"Any important questions?"

There was a silence.

Old Mr. Gupta the social science teacher shuffled in his seat. "Did the incident take place in the College grounds Father, sir."

The Head looked at old Mr. Gupta. "I don't see that it's important."

Mr. Gupta shuffled again. "Mr. D'Souza neither admitted or denied the allegation."

Father looked peeved. "That's right."

Mr. Gupta stood up. "Will you tell me please, whether it was in or out of the College?"

The Head nodded uncertainly.

"Then I suspect it was outside the College grounds. If that was the case, and the remark was illegal or the suggestion illegal it should have been reported to the police for enquiry."

He paused and looked around, then looked back at the Head who was obviously angry. "And as Mr. D'Souza was a senior staff and he had neither admitted or denied the charge —" he paused and leaned on the Head's table "— you acted unjustly and improperly. You have jeopardized the position of teachers in the future by such action. You have discredited what we teach the students about fair play and justice."

He stopped and looked around again. The Head was white with rage.

"I only have two years to retirement, I am not afraid to speak. I will tell you all again, as I have done hundreds of times. I'm a freedom fighter, I went to jail to ensure that the British type of justice would not prevail against our own people. I feel ashamed at the way this has gone about."

He sat down. A distinct murmur ran around the room. The Head sat motionless. Mrs. Mary William, an Anglo-Indian, said quietly, "Father, what Mr. D'Souza said or did may have been very bad, I don't know, but I have to agree with Mr. Gupta."

The Head stood up, he was visibly shaking. "I have said all I intend to say, good morning." He almost pushed his way through the staff and out of the room. The room fell silent. Mrs. William left first and everyone else followed.

Arun stood on the edge of the verandah, stunned. The bell rang. He walked with little interest to the class. He was shocked and numb.

It was a bigger shock several months later when the Christmas card Arun sent to S.M. was returned — with 'Return to Sender' scrawled across it in what Arun knew to be S.M.'s writing. He felt sad. He felt somehow used. He felt rejected. He felt depressed. He lay that night on the bed and felt salty tears run down his face.

Cleaning the Motorbikes

THE ALARM clock rang at five-thirty on Sunday morning. Arun got up quickly, and bathed with cold water to wake himself up.

He dressed quickly in casual clothing. He had promised the Head that he would spend an hour with the non-Christian boarding students while the Fathers were at early morning Sunday service. It was an annoying job that they all took turns at. Annoying to Arun because Sunday was about the only morning he had a chance to sleep in. An hour's duty always turned into two and it meant your Sunday was disjointed if you wanted to go anywhere early. He made himself tea and drank it standing in the kitchen. Everyone else was still sleeping, although he had heard a noise in his parents' bedroom.

Arun walked into the front room and was just about to unlatch the door when his father came in and looked surprised to see him. "Where are you going?"

Arun explained it all. "I'll be back by nine-thirty; I want to clean the motorbike this morning. It's last Sunday of the month too, so I suppose you want Chitti and me in the office?"

"Well I did want to talk to you, not necessarily about the accounts, I think they are alright this month. I will see you when you come back."

"Yes, but I do want to clean the bike."

His father nodded.

By excusing himself from having breakfast with the Fathers he got home at just half past nine. His mother fussed and made him sit and eat six iddli and chutney, and drink a glass of milk. She was in a talkative mood and he waited for the cleaning woman to ask something, then escaped to his bedroom. He put on his shorts, found some old rags in the bathroom scrap basket and started to clean the motorbike on the old side verandah. His father had purchased a new Ambassador and built a covered garage for it in the driveway. Arun and Chitti now had the old verandah almost to themselves for their motorbikes. Arun had taken his bike for servicing and it had come back dirty and oil-marked. He had already dirtied his new pants on oil flicking up from the chain. He was annoyed at the boys in the mechanic's shop for being so sloppy. Chitti came and sat on the step and starting to clean the front wheel of his machine.

"Can I tell you something, but you mustn't tell them I let you know?" Chitti had stopped cleaning and was looking at Arun. The words had been spoken rather quietly.

Arun looked up, "Sure, promise, what is it?"

"Jyothi told me first and then yesterday evening I heard it too, they are talking about your marriage. I think they have something going on. This morning Mom's expecting some of the Rotary women around for morning tea. It's supposed to be about the conference they are having. I reckon that one of the women will be the proposed mother-in-law."

He grinned. "You know Dad, cunning as a fox."

Arun stopped cleaning the stainless-steel pedal bracket. "Do I have any say in all this?"

Chitti grinned at him. "Sure you do, as always, just say 'Yes' and accept it. Who are we to speak!"

"And if I don't want to get married?"

Chitti changed his voice. "Please take the next bus to Varanasi and become a sadhu."

They laughed together.

Their father walked in, all dressed in white and looking like he was a Chief Minister. He stood and watched them. He started a conversation with both of them about business. That led to life and security and future.

Chitti looked sideways at Arun, they both knew the conversation format. He was about to get round to some major point. Arun felt his stomach quiver. Their father called the servant girl for water and a chair. He drank the water and sat himself in the chair, being careful not to crease his pants.

"Arun —" Arun looked up and then back at the chain he was cleaning with an old toothbrush. "It's about time you thought about marriage, you are old enough and nicely settled in a good job. All you need now is a good wife. There is plenty of room here in this house. It would be good for all of us."

Silence. Arun had decided to let his father talk.

"You are the eldest, so we need to think about it seriously."

Silence.

"What do you say, isn't it about the right time?"

Arun kept on cleaning the chain, maybe looking even more intently at the job he was doing. Without looking up he said, "No."

Silence.

"No what?"

"No to what you just said." Arun kept on cleaning. "If Chitti wants to get married he can, I'm sure that whoever you are contracting will be good enough for him."

His father shifted in the chair. "Don't talk nonsense. How can Chitti babu get married, he is only a boy still, and anyway the eldest son has to get married first, that's tradition."

He called for more water. A sure sign that he was getting agitated.

"Thought you said that all this tradition and stuff was what was holding the development of India back. Caste and rituals and all that stuff. You used to always rubbish it before. What made you change? How come we are all of a sudden traditionalist."

The water arrived and he drank it in one gulp.

"Look don't talk that College rubbish. You know I only want you to have what's good for you. The girl will be as good as your mother. Better I suppose because she will be properly educated and know things."

"If you only want what is good for me, then please do what is best for me." Arun looked at his father who started to smile. "And what's best for me is to not arrange my marriage. I'm not interested. I don't want to argue. You want the best. I'm telling you what I want. So let's leave it at that."

The grin had left Chitti's face and the smile on their father's face had disappeared just as suddenly.

"Alright, I'll build you a separate house."

"My room is exactly what I want. I don't need a house because I'm not getting married."

There was a silence.

"Ahh, I know it, you already have a girlfriend and you want to marry her, and not who we decide on, that's the truth isn't it? Isn't it. You have a bit on the side already. Answer me."

Arun stood up and walked to the other side of the motorbike. "Alright I'll answer you. I'm not getting married for another five years. I'm not even going to make a promise now either."

"Five years. Look don't think you are so big that you can challenge me. I'm head of this family and I make these decisions. It's almost summer. I'm telling you that not five years, not five months, but in five weeks you will be married. That's final and I don't want any more nonsense talk. Do you hear me."

Arun stood and faced his father. "I heard you," he paused and took a deep breath, "but I don't and won't agree. Please don't make arrangements that will make you and Mother look foolish. I am telling you that what's best for me is not to be married."

His father walked up to the other side of the motorbike. "And I'm telling you that in five weeks it will all be over. Married, settled, happy."

"Dad." Chitti spoke for the first time.

A thundering "What!" came from their father.

"You know Arun has always listened to you. He has always done what you ask. He has never made the type of problems for you that I have, you know, with my drinking and this and that. Don't you think that this time you should listen to him. He might have his reasons. Don't push him, Dad."

Their father had gone redder and redder in the face as Chitti spoke.

"Don't push him! I'll push him harder than he can dream about if he dares question me one more time about this. It's settled. *Don't push him!*"

The last three words were almost spat out with anger. With that he lifted his foot and pushed the motorbike towards Arun. It toppled and as Arun reached out to grab the handlebar it slid on an oil spill. The gear pedal caught his ankle and he slipped and fell. As he looked up Chitti grabbed the bike. He saw his father walk inside. Arun stood up quickly but his ankle pained him terribly. Chitti pulled the bike back on its stand. He was standing on the other side, just staring in disbelief at Arun. He looked towards the door and shook his head. Arun nodded. He was close to tears, with anger and pain. He smiled quickly at Chitti and walked with a limp to his room. He sat on the edge of the water tank and put his ankle into the cold water.

Chitti came in a few minutes later with a glass of water and a glass of tea.

Arun drank the water and took the tea from Chitti. "Chitti, I know you mean well, I appreciate what you said, but stay out of this argument. You can't take my side and win. You can't take my side and remain friends with him. If you side with me, he will make life unbearable for you too. You know he will."

Chitti stared at him. "Why don't you want to get married, brother?"

They looked at each other. Arun didn't know what to say. Chitti was waiting for an answer.

"I simply just don't want to get married. I'm happy single. I don't need a wife. I don't want that responsibility."

Arun paused and leaned over to rub his ankle still in the water. He was uncertain what to really say to Chitti. He looked up and smiled at Chitti. "I am me. I have my books, my music, my sports, my job, and I don't want a wife too."

Chitti shrugged his shoulders. "You are right. I'm not going to get involved. Trying to explain all that to him would be like trying to get a rat to understand no matter how big its cock was, it still couldn't run up the leg of an elephant and fuck it."

Arun could hardly believed what Chitti had said. Chitti grinned and they both laughed.

"You got a better way of expressing it?"

Arun shook his head and Chitti turned to leave. "Arun, I wish you luck brother, lots of it. You will need it."

Arun got dressed and walked out through the back lane, slowly, his ankle still paining. He waited for a rickshaw to come along. He took the rickshaw to the Post Office and walked to the side window where the telegraph office was. It was open on Sundays, ten to twelve and four to seven.

He sent a telegram to Abdullah:

HAVE MARRIAGE PROPOSAL PROBLEM AT
HOME WILL COME TO SEE YOU FRIDAY
NIGHT STOP CONFUSED NEED ADVICE ARUN

He then took a rickshaw around to John's; he needed to be out of the house. The whole of the family were there. It was one of Sam's children's birthdays. Arun stayed there until evening.

As he left John said, "Having big problems with the contractor or what?"

Arun nodded, "Yes, I just screwed one of the contractor's major plans up."

John raised his eyebrows.

The next week was terrible. He and his father avoided each other. Arun didn't go to Rotaract because he knew his father was also attending the meeting to discuss community work for building a bus shelter. His mother kept asking him questions. All subtle, she thought, but Arun saw through them. He knew by the way she asked that she was asking them because his father had told her to.

On Thursday he said, "Mom, shut up about it please. I'll tell you what I really think sometime next week. Maybe Tuesday. Please get off it."

They were both sitting on the front verandah. He was marking geometry exam papers. She was just sitting. "I'm also going to Hyderabad on Friday night. So please get the dhobi to be on time. You can make me a packet of halva too."

She looked at him and smiled. "See you do need a wife." She paused and quickly looked around and lowered her voice. "Your father thinks that you go to Hyderabad because you have a girl-friend there. What's she like?"

Arun pushed all the papers together and stood up. "Wrong, wrong, wrong. Don't worry about making the halva either, and I'll shout at the dhobi myself thank you."

He felt sorry about the way he spoke to her. He had never shouted like this at her. They looked at each other. She looked away. He walked off.

Visiting Abdullah

AN HOUR before the train was due on Friday evening Chitti came into his room. "As everyone knows that you are going to Hyderabad to see your girlfriend, do you want me to drop you at the station, or will you humbly go by rickshaw? The halva is made too. A whole biscuit tin of it. Enough to feed a harem, not just one girl friend."

Arun sighed and closed his case. He looked around the room and nearly left without his ticket and reservation slip.

The train was on time. Chitti waved and left as soon as he was in the bogey. Arun swapped bunks with a young guy. He took the top one and climbed up and went to sleep. He was tired, and mentally exhausted. The tension in the house had really drained him. His ankle still pained and he had an elastic bandage wrapped over it.

At Secunderabad Arun looked out to see if Abdullah had come there to meet him. Arun wasn't sure if it would be easier to get to Abdullah's place from Secunderabad or Hyderabad station. They spotted each other and waved. Arun stayed seated, and Abdullah came along.

"Get down here. My place is closer to here than Hyderabad. I've got the bike. You got much luggage?"

Arun grinned. "One case and one biscuit tin full of halva."

They walked through the station and out to his motorbike. They strapped the tin and case on the back luggage rack.

"You will never believe this, but we are going to a little party, just six people I think. I was already invited, and had accepted when your telegram arrived. I phoned the guy and explained. I phoned him again this evening and said we might come direct from the station and that you might want to change your clothes there. He said no problem."

Arun looked and smiled at Abdullah. "What's all this about!"

"Get on."

They rode down the highway, turned off at the lake junction and eventually came to a large housing estate with four sets of four-storey flats.

"It's the flat up on the fourth floor where those coloured lights are hanging over the balcony."

Arun was off the bike and Abdullah pulled it onto its stand.

"Well it goes like this. Three weeks ago I was feeling very sexy. I walked down to the river gardens. Not to pick up anyone, just to look at the scene. It's the place where guys meet. I was sitting on the wall," he laughed, "eating an icecream as it happened."

Abdullah started to undo the rope to get the case and tin off. "Anyway to make a long story short, I got talking to this guy. He is a pilot doing some training here for Air India. We didn't have it off or anything, but we became kind of friends straight away. I've been to his place a few times and he comes around to my house. This morning two other pilots came from Calcutta and he wanted to have a party for them. They are all the same — I mean like us. Two other local guys are coming that he knows too."

Arun was silent. He couldn't believe it. Still Abdullah must be telling the truth. Arun had no idea Abdullah knew other guys like themselves. He hadn't thought about it like that.

They were the last to arrive. The guy who had the flat was very friendly and made them feel really welcome. He and the other two pilots looked the same age as Abdullah. The other two were from a bank. One was only about twenty and the other looked about Arun's age. The older bank guy was rather effeminate.

Sanjay the host showed Arun the bathroom. He unlocked his case and took out clean clothing and a towel. As he walked into the bathroom Ajay the older bank guy called out., "Leave the door open. Then if you faint we won't have to break the door down to give you mouth-to-cock resuscitation."

The only thing Arun could think of saying was, "Maybe I'd faint if you did it!"

Ajay laughed. "More likely I'd choke."

A few minutes later the taller of the pilots, Vinod, called out, "Want me to check your undercarriage."

Praveen the other pilot added, "I'll check your joystick if you want me to."

The party went on for hours. Sanjay drank a couple of beers. Arun had a brandy with ice and soda; he thought it tasted terrible. Abdullah and Sanjay stuck to orange juice with lime. The two guys from the bank drank whisky. They pushed the chairs against the wall and sat on the floor to eat. Arun sat next to Ajay, who caught him looking at him. Actually he wasn't looking as much as he was smelling. Ajay had some kind of perfume on.

"First I put on some of that Musk aftershave. Then I felt daring so put some of my wife's perfume on. Doesn't mix very well does it!"

He sounded slightly drunk. Everyone laughed.

"God I wish I wasn't married. It's supposed to make you happy but it's the silliest thing I ever agreed to," Ajay said to no one in particular.

"Did you actually agree?" Praveen asked.

"No, I just went along like a lamb to the slaughterhouse."

He turned to Arun, "Are you married?"

Arun shook his head.

"If you are gay like us, believe you me, don't. Run away from home like a little boy, but don't get married." He paused.

Ravi, who had spoken little all night, said quietly, "I agreed because I was frightened what people would say if I refused. I knew that if I had told my parents it would have been —" He paused, picked up the glass and washed his hand in the plate. "It would have been... well just too much for my parents. My sister returned home with her two kids and is saying she is going to get a divorce. She already has a job in an office. My parents think it's disgraceful. They keep telling her to either go back or get her own place. She refuses both. Told them that as they had arranged it, then they too should suffer with her. Her husband drinks like a fish, beats her. Shouts at the children. Animal."

Sanjay came around with special percolated coffee. He handed everyone some of the halva Arun had brought with him.

"If I didn't have this job, and was away so much, well I don't know what I'd do. Really my wife is a first-class person. She really is. That's not the point though is it? I don't love her. I know she feels it. I'm sure she doesn't know I'm gay, but I'm also sure she knows I fuck her only because it's duty and all that shit."

Arun listened with fascination to what they were saying. He had never been with a group of guys like this. He didn't even know that there were such groups and parties.

Praveen was sitting next to Abdullah. He turned slightly to him. "If you don't mind me asking, how come you're not married? I mean, if you don't mind my saying so, I thought Muslims had to promise marriage when they had their foreskins cut off."

Abdullah laughed until tears almost ran down his face. Everyone laughed with him.

"I'll tell you all I could do when they cut it off was faint. It was a terrible disgrace."

He paused. "At College I met a guy, knew him for years. We kind of discovered each other. I really loved him deeply. It helped me to understand what I am — *a man who loves men.* I resolved then never to be forced to marry. Sadly the guy died. It hurt me deeply for a long time. My father tried a marriage contract on me. I told him I liked to fuck little boys, and that it was best I leave home. He questioned, raved and ranted. Threatened me. Everything imaginable. I left home. We don't communicate much nowadays."

Abdullah and Arun were the first to leave. Abdullah had a small old house in the Muslim quarter with an open courtyard at the side. Inside the courtyard however was an ultra-modern building which looked a bit like a greenhouse. Abdullah showed him quickly through the house and they went into the kitchen where Abdullah made them coffee. The kitchen had every modern convenience imaginable. It looked like something from a Western interior decoration magazine.

Abdullah asked quietly, with a grin, "Interesting night? Interesting party?"

Arun smiled back and raised his eyebrows. "Incredible. It's beyond my imagination. I've never been to a party like that. I just didn't know such groups even existed. Fantastic."

Abdullah rinsed the cups and Arun followed him back into the sitting room. One of the few old things in the house, a large grandfather clock, chimed.

"Cinderella time." Abdullah said, picking up Arun's case and took his case into the bedroom. "I didn't really know there were groups like tonight's either until I came to live here. Meeting Sanjay kind of confirmed a few ideas and suspicions I had that such things went on."

They both yawned and looked slyly at each other. Abdullah stretched out his hand, Arun took it and Abdullah squeezed him warmly.

"Let's talk tomorrow, I really need some action now, I'm starved."

Abdullah grinned, "Alright, I'll give you something to nibble on."

Arun didn't remember falling asleep but he remembered feeling content and satisfied being cuddled by Abdullah. He knew what his preferences were. They slept late, got up and ate a lazy breakfast.

In the late afternoon, just as the breeze started, they sat in the open courtyard. It had been a hot day for early summer. The jasmine creepers along the side of the house were loaded with flowers. The perfumed smell filled the garden.

Abdullah got up to answer the knock on the gate. Two small girls came in to collect flowers. They took a cloth-covered dish from their basket first and placed it on the table Abdullah and Arun were sitting at. Abdullah untied it as the girls watched. Before he lifted the lid he pretended to smell the dish.

"Samosa with tamarind and clove chutney."

The little girl clapped her hands with delight and said in Urdu, "You always guess right, Uncle."

The three of them clapped hands together and laughed. Arun enjoyed watching them.

"They collect the flowers every afternoon for their mother, aunty and grandmother. They are second nieces to me. Their aunt sends me the samosa every week — 'as payment', as she puts it."

After the girls had left Arun realized that the scent in the air had changed. He looked around and saw that in the far corner was a pink magnolia tree in bloom. Behind that was a well-kept rose garden. Abdullah watched him inspecting.

"If you were not here I would have been in the garden all day, it's my hobby. I work hard all week, and the leather smell gets to me some weeks. The garden is my escape from it all."

They sat quietly for a while, just sipping their sweet lime drinks and eating the samosa, watching the little mynah birds hopping through the garden. Abdullah stretched himself in the chair, folded his legs and arms and turned towards Arun.

"I don't want to tell you what to do. You have to make the final decision. Ultimately you have to live with your own decision.

Whatever you decide I'll always be your friend."

Arun then realized that Abdullah was looking at him intently.

"But I want to tell you about something that happened a few years back — something that changed my life. Made me think differently. Made me make decisions about my life for myself. My rights." He paused, and seemed to look around. "It's a story that makes me very sad too. Sam, your friend John's brother knows it. Sam shared part of the story and the sadness too. In a different way, but it hurt him too."

"Is it something about Venkatramu's son, the one that died of brain fever? I went to his marriage. John told me he had died suddenly and that Sam was upset for months. He became quite depressed about it."

Abdullah nodded, "Yes, Venkatramu's son Shivaji."

When Abdullah finished he had tears running down his face. The sun had gone down, the sky was a dull grey pink. The mynah birds had all flown off. The breeze had dropped.

Arun stood up and went into the kitchen and made coffee. He felt a new kind of sadness. A sadness he had never experienced before.

The Tragedy

WHEN SHIVA and his wife were finally left alone in the newly painted and furnished room both lay on the bed, smiled at each other and fell asleep fully dressed.

When Shiva woke up he heard Radha in the bathroom. He felt tired still and had a slight headache. He smiled though. He still had his marriage gear on. Radha came out and smiled and sat on the bed. He went in and bathed and dressed in clean clothes and they went out into the front room to be greeted by his father who immediately took them into the puja room and lit the lamps and incense.

The day seemed to be almost a miniature of yesterday. They were shunted here and there. People came and went, and they had no privacy at all.

Radha had served him and then his father and all the male members of the immediate family at lunchtime. It wasn't until he started to eat that he realized he was very hungry. He and Radha hadn't really eaten anything much the day before. That night they were able to excuse themselves after supper, both telling the truth in pleading headaches. Radha searched through her bag and found a small jar of herbal balm. She rubbed some on her forehead and offered it to Shiva. She rubbed it into his neck.

Shiva tried to block everything from his mind and just concentrate on getting hard. It worked for a bit and then seemed to go flat. He caressed Radha and she responded. He got to the point of being hard enough to try and enter. Radha winced with pain. He felt her fingers dig into his back. Somehow it made him go flat again.

"I'm sorry, it's just painful. I shouldn't have complained like that, please do it again. It will only pain the first time, my sister said," Radha whispered to him.

Tired, he said, "Sorry I don't know what's wrong, I must be too..."

The next night he gave up the idea of concentrating and thought of his first experience with Sam. The mental picture of Sam's curved cock made him hard, and he felt excited. Radha had rubbed cream on him very shyly. She pulled him to her and he slowly moved in. He knew she was in pain but he kept going. He knew that she was supposed to climax like him. Nothing seemed to happen for her and he couldn't stop. He let himself go. When he withdrew and turned onto his side he saw that the sheet was bloodstained. Almost like a film he had seen many years ago. Radha was very embarrassed.

"Don't worry about it please," he said.

She rolled him off the bed and pulled the sheet off and took it into the bathroom. He heard her washing it in the bucket. He didn't remember anything else. He fell asleep before she returned. He had strange and frightening dreams.

When he woke in the morning Radha wasn't there. He bathed and dressed and walked through the house. Radha was in the kitchen with Shanti and his mother. They were in whispering conversation that stopped as soon as he came in. Radha stood up and fetched a stool for him into the front room, getting him out of the kitchen.

The day went boringly by. In the afternoon he and Ramu sat on the verandah.

"I saw Abdullah this morning. I told him we might meet him this evening for tiffin somewhere in the centre. I suppose we can escape for half an hour."

Shiva nodded.

"What's wrong?" Ramu asked.

Shiva didn't answer, just shrugged his shoulders.

"Don't worry, you will get the hang of it soon."

They got just thirty minutes' leave from his mother. She wasn't happy about him leaving in case he didn't come back in time for the night puja. He promised her he would. Ramu double-promised. Radha avoided looking at him. He imagined that his mother and sister had made comments about 'men always going out'. It had been part of the lunchtime conversation the men heard from the kitchen as they ate.

Abdullah was waiting for them. They had tea and salt biscuits at the Diamond Teashop. Abdullah tried to get Shiva into conversation but he didn't respond very much. Abdullah asked if they could escape and go to the cinema.

Shiva shook his head. Ramu said, "He can't but I sure can. See you in twenty minutes. I'm going to make sure he gets home and is accounted for, then I'm going to the toilet and escaping. I've been in that temple enough in the last week to keep me going for another month or longer."

Abdullah laughed. "You guys think you get it bad, why don't you take up being a Muslim and then you would have something to complain about. My father thinks we should all go at least five times a day."

Ramu called a rickshaw and he and Shiva climbed in.

Abdullah said, "See you."

Shiva smiled at him. The first smile Abdullah had seen on him for weeks. "Goodbye," he said quietly and touched Ab's hand.

By supper time Shiva felt sick. He knew he would have to try and go through it again tonight. But how could he go on having to think about Sam and them fucking the prostitute together to get an erection to try and satisfy his wife! It was crazy. How did he get himself into this mess? How could he have been so stupid to have allowed them to do this to him? He had just accepted it all. He had not argued one word. He knew it wasn't for him and now he had spoiled his life and Radha's. It was so unfair on her and him.

He would close his eyes this time and think of Abdullah. He did and it worked. Well, kind of worked. He did get an erection and he did keep it and it did go in and he did ejaculate. But he was so tense that he knew Radha hadn't really enjoyed it.

He mumbled, "Sorry."

Radha smiled. "It's alright, we don't have to be perfect to start with."

He kissed her lightly on the lips.

The next morning he slept late again and found Radha had already bathed and left their rooms. He was feeling pretty depressed.

There was a knock at the door.

"Come in," he called.

It was Radha and Shanti. Both looked rather serious.

"Radha is very embarrassed to tell you this. She has to go home for a few days." Shanti paused.

Shiva was confused. It must have shown on his face.

"Her monthly time has come on suddenly. She should go home this first time and come back when it's over."

Shiva didn't know what to say. He also felt embarrassed.

Radha packed a few of her things into a case and Shanti took it out. Radha stood and smiled. "We always seem to be saying sorry to each other. I'll try to be quick and return."

Shiva stepped towards her and held her hands. "Goodbye," he whispered and kissed her on the cheek.

He stayed in his room for an hour and his mother came with breakfast. She didn't say anything, just put the plates on the small table.

Ramu had shifted into the small upper room at the far end of the house. He didn't particularly like this as it was right in line with the temple P.A. speaker. Shiva wandered along to the room. Ramu wasn't there. He waited until he knew his father wouldn't be around and took the newspaper from the stool. Ramu came in at lunchtime.

"I've got three days' leave. I think I'll go home tonight."

Shiva had secretly been thinking that maybe he would be able to talk to Ramu about how he felt. He had thought he would like to have sex with him too. Maybe it would put things in balance. He was confused.

After lunch he followed Ramu to his room. He felt somehow that Ramu didn't want to talk. He felt that Ramu also didn't want to have it with him either. Nothing was said but he felt it.

Ramu packed his small bag and Shiva walked out with him. Shiva called a rickshaw and went with Ramu to the bus complex. The express was there. Ramu rushed to get a seat. Shiva waited for the bus to pull out and waved goodbye. He walked through the main market, purchased a couple of things and went to the afternoon cinema. When he reached home only the cook was there cleaning pots. She told him that his father was looking for him and that they had all gone to puja early because it was full-moon day.

Shiva went into the puja room and lit the oil lamp for his Nataraj. He lit extra incense sticks and watched them burn. He went to his room, bathed, dressed again and went back to the puja room. The oil lamp had gone out. He relit it.

It was hot and no breeze was blowing when the family came out of the temple. Their father led the way. He had a large, long-handled iron spoon full of embers. He went into the house and walked towards the puja room.

No one followed him in with it and its trailing smoke. They sat on the verandah and called the woman to bring them water. Shanti watched her father going into the house and laughed. "Looks like an old steam train with all that smoke."

Her mother laughed and hit her lightly upon the shoulder. "Don't let him hear you say that."

Shiva's father was annoyed when he walked into the puja room. The light was turned off. The oil lamp was smoking and casting shadows on the wall. He started to walk around the small sanctum. The shadow on the wall confused him. He focused his eyes and gasped and dropped the spoon with the embers. He couldn't breathe. He clutched his chest and groaned.

"Go and see what he has done. Sounds like he dropped the embers. I hope he hasn't burnt his hand."

Her eldest son frowned and slowly stood up. He walked into the puja room and saw his father lying on the ground. He rushed to him, and lifted his head. He knew that something terrible was wrong. He laid his head down and stood up.

He turned and nearly fainted. He now saw what his father had seen. It was Shivaji, hanging from the puja room beam.

He felt urine running down his leg. He couldn't get the words to come out of his mouth. He wanted to scream but his mouth just opened and closed. He felt numb all over. He heard his mother call, "What's wrong?"

Telling the Truth

THE TRAIN from Hyderabad was late getting into Chintana. Arun knew that he would have to be quick to get home, bathe, and be at College on time. In fact he wanted to be there early this Monday morning. He had a plan that needed immediate action.

His weekend with Abdullah had made everything clear for him. He knew what he had to do. Had to do if he was to remain free, and maybe sane too.

He was happy to see that the car had gone when he arrived home. His father had already left for work. Chitti's motorbike was gone too. He rushed into the house and greeted his mother. Told her he had a good weekend and explained he had to rush. She wasn't at all talkative and he was glad of that. He hadn't wanted to be sharp with her again.

He rode the motorbike along the back lane and around the sports ground. He rarely took this short cut. He waited for Mrs. Sen to arrive at the library. Mrs. Sen was not only librarian but also the College staff banker — she did all of their bank work if staff banked with either SBI or OIB. In addition she was a constant source of houses and rooms for staff. Her husband ran a mixed agency and made commissions on organizing rentals and leases.

After the usual Monday morning greetings Arun asked, "I'm in urgent need of a small place to rent. One or two rooms, and its own toilet and bathroom."

"Oh Mr. Arun, my sister's husband just repainted the second unit at their place. You know it don't you, down on the Tank Road."

Arun nodded. It was exactly what he needed. He couldn't wish for more. Last year's relief teacher who he got to know well had lived there. He took out his wallet and gave her five hundred rupees.

"I'll take it. No question. Tell me how much you need later. Would you also draw this money for me."

He gave her a withdrawal form and signed it. She had his passbook. He wanted two thousand rupees in cash. He knew he would be spending money this week.

Mrs. Sen nodded. "I'll phone my sister-in-law and tell her. You can pick up the key and speak to them this afternoon. Is that alright?"

He nodded. Students were starting to come into the library.

The day went slowly. After College he went straight home. In the storeroom he found what he wanted, an old wooden chest. He packed it with books. He rode round to see the small house unit.

They were expecting him. It was freshly decorated and still had the paint smell. It was only five minutes to the College by motorbike. He explained he would send a rickshaw with his books. They were happy to put it into the room if he didn't arrive back by the time the rickshaw got there. He managed two trips with the trunk without anyone really noticing what he was doing. The girls were still at their tutor's, Chitti was out with his father, and his mother was engrossed in making sweets for the Rotary meeting that night.

On Tuesday morning he heard his father talking in the kitchen so he stepped out by the side lane and took tea at the corner. He came back through the front gate and his father immediately confronted him.

"You told your mother that on Tuesday you would give a clear answer about our marriage plans for you. Today is Tuesday. Sit down."

His father said all this very quietly but the quietness didn't fool Arun. He knew that he was in an 'attack' mood. Mother came out with tea. The girls were making last-minute rushes here and there to go off to morning tuition and school. The rickshaw was already waiting. They dashed out waving and shouting. Chitti's motorbike was gone so he imagined he was on a site somewhere.

"What have you got to say?" his father said sipping his tea. Mother had wisely disappeared into the back kitchen.

"I'm sorry to disappoint you, but I'm not getting married."

"Why not?" His father put the tea down. "Just a simple answer, no complications."

Arun sat more upright in his chair. "Because I'm not interested in marriage. I don't intend to get married."

His father was looking straight ahead and not at him. "Why not?"

Arun drew in a deep breath. *"Because I am a man that prefers men."*

His father sat still: his next sentence somehow surprised Arun. "You prefer men to women."

Silence.

"That means you are a *chamma chacka* then."

"You know that's not true, you know I never wear anything other than men's clothing. Don't make it something it's not. I just don't want to get married because my sexual preference are for men not women."

A long deep silence came between them.

"Then you can't live here. I will disown you. I won't and can't accept this business. I know now what you are. It disgusts me. I think if I stood up now I would kill you. My own son is one of those."

He looked at Arun with disgust. "Who else knows this, other than your other sick friends?"

Arun felt calm. "No one."

"How can you teach at the College when you say you are one of them?"

"I don't know what you mean by 'one of them' — I've said I'm not an 'evening person'. I just have different feelings. Working at the College has no connection."

He paused and turned more towards his father. "Can I try to explain?"

"No!"

"If you think I fuck schoolboys, or they fuck me, you are wrong."

His father stood up and sat down again.

"I won't have you in the house, you are not my son if you insist on saying these things. I will even go to the Head and tell him what you are. Then we will see what you have to say. What will you do then?"

"It's really none of his business."

"We'll see." He looked carefully at Arun, "I will ask you one more time."

Arun didn't wait for him to ask. "I'm sorry Father, I'm not getting married."

He stood up and walked out of the gate to the corner. He stood for a few minutes, went back, collected his bag and pushed the motorbike out of the gate. He had known this would happen. He felt unbelievably calm. He knew that a storm was coming. He knew his father well enough to know that he was vengeful when crossed. Arun had crossed him.

He was in the middle of the second class for the morning. The Head's peon came in and whispered, "Father wants to see you immediately."

Arun put work on the board and gave a couple of short instructions to the class.

At the administration office Brother Victor was sitting outside the Head's office typing as always. "Go in, he is waiting for you."

Arun felt his pocket to check again that he had the papers there. The Head was sitting upright as a pole with his hands on the desk. Arun's father was in the visitor's chair on the right side, sitting just as upright. Arun was not asked to sit.

"Your father has just told me that you have refused to get married."

"Yes, that's correct, Father."

"The reason why, he also told me and I am deeply shocked. I can't believe it though. Is it true?"

Arun looked straight at the Head. "If my father told you then it must be correct. What did he say?"

The Head leaned back. He spoke in a lowered voice. "He said that you are," he paused, "a homosexual."

Arun said in the same voice, "I don't like that word, I prefer to simply say that I'm a man who prefers the total company of men, emotionally and physically."

There was a silence except for the sound of Brother Victor's typing in the next room through the closed door.

"Same thing," the Head said quietly as though it was a disease. "I'm afraid that we can't have such people teaching in the College."

He heard his father shuffle his feet.

"Father, I have never had a relationship with any of the students, that is not my interest."

"I can't accept you continuing to work as a teacher when you say that."

"I don't expect you to understand such things." Arun took out the two letters from his pocket. "Here is my leave letter as of now, together with my resignation. Kindly have my dues finalized with the bursar on Friday. I am sorry that it has ended this way, Father. I have great love for the College and the staff and yourself. I don't agree with you on this, but I understand. Goodbye."

The Head nodded. Arun turned so as not to look at his father, or the man who used to be his father, and walked out. He had told the truth. A price had to be paid.

The gate was open and he rode the motorbike onto the front verandah. Chitti was sitting at the small table he often used, a set of plans spread out in front of him.

"How come you are home at this hour, don't tell me another students' or teachers' strike, you lot hardly ever work." He grinned. "Not like when I was a student."

"Nothing wrong, I suppose. I've just taken leave for..." He paused. "Chitti, you better come and listen to me, I've resigned actually."

Chitti stood up suddenly, put weights on the papers and followed him. Arun went in and started to pack the last of his things.

"I told Dad that I wouldn't get married. He asked why, and I told him. He went to the Head and told him, and I resigned. You had better get ready for a bit of a shock. If you don't accept what I say, that's alright, I'll understand. The truth is Chitti that I'm not interested in marriage. I prefer to have relations with men. I just happen to be a man who loves men."

Chitti was leaning against the door. "You mean you are," he paused, "you mean a homo."

"That's a foreign brand name Chitti. I don't like it, but o.k. it's one way to describe me."

Chitti sat down on the step and grinned, "Wow, I've got a brother who's a homo. You aren't a *chamma chakka* though are you. Shit I hope not."

Now Arun grinned. "No, I'm just a normal guy. I live and act normal, except for my sexual preference." He stopped, "And Chitti I don't think it's abnormal to have these preferences. I just happen to be in the minority that's all."

"I know a few good homo jokes, but I don't suppose this is the time to tell them."

They laughed together.

"Wow, wait until I tell Vasu, he thinks he is king with a sister living at home separated from her husband and demanding a divorce. They told her to leave but she refuses. She said that they had arranged her marriage to an animal guy and now they too can share the problems with her."

Chitti looked up at Arun. "You remember that boy Sharat that lived opposite a few years ago. His father was the Assistant Station Master. When we were in tenth class and studying together we used to handpump each other." He paused, "You ever been sucked?"

Arun nodded.

"Well Sharat sucked me a few times. I thought it was great. He wanted me to suck him, but I refused. He never cleaned his cock properly and it smelt."

He reached out and took a glass of water from the clay pot. "I supposed I grew out of it."

Arun smiled at the statement. "It was just a stage in your growing-up. I grew up with a different preference. I have a friend who knows a guy that never had any relationship with another guy until he was twenty-five. The point of a boy having homosexual relations or experiences during his growing-up years has nothing to do with what his long-term preference is."

"What are you going to do brother?" It was a question with concern in its tone.

"Well I'm leaving here, Father doesn't want me in the house. He has disowned me. No problem. I will stay in Chintana for a while. I'm not sure. Just make a new life for myself."

Their mother came in. "What's happening?"

The two brothers looked at each other. Chitti said, "Arun had a big argument with Dad and he is going away for a few days. He's not in a mood to discuss it now. I'll tell you all about it when you come back at lunchtime."

She nodded. She was going to the hospital for sugar tests. After she had left Chitti said, "I'll tell her as soon as she comes back, before Dad has a chance to make you into some kind of sex maniac. You aren't a sex maniac are you?"

"Well I think sometimes when I'm in bed I am."

They both burst into laughter.

"I don't care, you are my brother. I will always support you, no matter what."

Chitti turned and left the room. He stood at the door and said,

"Thanks for telling me the truth. That's important. I appreciate it."

V. June 1993

GEET WAS in Madras buying the first computer for the students of Arun's Tutorial Institute.

Arun lay on his bed with the air-cooler blasting him. It was a hot Sunday morning. He had one objective for the day and it was to do nothing.

He heard the gate click. He hoped it wasn't a student. He looked up as the footsteps reached the door. "Yes, come in."

The door opened slowly. It was a young woman. He sat up with surprise. She smiled at him and came in. It was his sister Jyothi. She looked beautiful in a green silk sari with jasmine tied in her hair. He sat up and she immediately sat on the bed next to him. They hadn't met since he left home. Chitti had called every month and chatted, but his sisters were forbidden. Chitti ignored such stupid rules of his father's. The girls couldn't.

"How are you Jyothi?"

She grinned and took his hand. "I'm well." She adjusted her saree. "Dad wants me to get married soon. I've seen the boy. He is quite nice too. Works in the Tasildhars office. He is a graduate. There is a small problem though."

She looked at Arun directly. "I've refused to marry him unless I can invite you, and only if you come."

She paused and smiled and bit her lip and looked down at her lap. "You can bring your friend too if you want."

Arun sat still listening intently. He couldn't believe it.

"Dad of course is throwing fits and threatening me, scolding Mom, raving on and being his big-time self as usual." She laughed. "I packed my case a few days back and told him that I'd run away to Hyderabad and become a prostitute if he kept on raving."

She paused and smiled at Arun, flicking her hair off her eyes. "He has been quiet for two days. Last night he started again and Chitti told him that he would not go to the marriage either. Will you come?"

"What's Baby say about it all?"

"Baby says nothing. She refuses to take sides and that's making him mad too."

"And Mother?"

Jyothi looked at Arun with surprise on her face, "You don't know, Chitti didn't tell you?"

"Tell me what, Jyothi?"

"Mother hasn't spoken to Dad since the day Chitti told her about you when you left. She doesn't speak to him. She goes nowhere with him. Refuses to even give him a glass of water. The only word she speaks to him when he drives her crazy is to call him a 'Rotarpig' — he hates it. Mother says that he did what he wanted in life. She said to all of us in front of him about her and him having sex before their marriage. She told us how he used to go to prostitutes every time she was pregnant. Oh dear, she really blames him for you losing your job and leaving home."

"Don't you think that it would be better if I didn't come. It would only be — well, complicated — embarrassing."

"If you don't want me to get married, then don't come. I'd only be embarrassed," she stopped and smiled, "well, if you came in a saree."

She threw her arms around him and they laughed and laughed.

Arun walked with her to the gate. He watched her get into the rickshaw and waved.

* * *

The Gay Men's Press Collection

Many of the most popular titles from our backlist are now being reissued in The Gay Men's Press Collection series. These currently include:

Michael Davidson
THE WORLD, THE FLESH, AND MYSELF
In the heyday of the foreign correspondent, Michael Davidson travelled the globe and campaigned against oppression and injustice. Bravely writing in 1962 "the life story of a lover of boys", his autobiography, praised by Arthur Koestler, is a classic memoir of gay life in the first half of the century.

ISBN 0 907040 63 2   UK £12.95 US $19.95 AUS $24.95

Michael Davidson
SOME BOYS
The still more revealing sequel to *The World, The Flesh and Myself*, showing an unerring personal empathy with boys from four continents and four decades.

ISBN 0 85449 259 3   UK £8.95 US $14.95 AUS $17.95

Richie McMullen
ENCHANTED YOUTH
This follow-up to *Enchanted Boy*, a "journey through abuse to prostitution", finds Richie escaping Liverpol at fifteen for a life on the game in London's West End. Though preyed on by criminal gangs, rent boys give each other comfort and support, in the excitement that was Soho in the rock'n'roll years.

ISBN 0 85449 134 1   UK £7.95 US $12.95 AUS $17.95

The Gay Men's Press Collection

James Purdy
NARROW ROOMS
A cult book that Derek Jarman planned to film, this "dark and splendid affair by an authentic American genius" (Gore Vidal) is a shattering novel of sexual passion in the remote Appalachians, and a journey into the dark night of the American soul.
ISBN 0 907040 57 8   *UK £7.95 US $12.95 AUS $17.95*

David Rees
THE MILKMAN'S ON HIS WAY
In the early 1980s, this best-selling coming-out novel broke new ground as a positive image of growing up gay. "The best fictional guide for gay youth that has yet appeared" (*Identity*). " A more convincing portrayal of gay coming-of-age isn't to be had" (*Mister*).
ISBN 0 907040 12 8   *UK £6.95 US $10.95 AUS $14.95*

Christopher Bram
SURPRISING MYSELF
Joel and Corey are two young men trying to build a life together in New York, amid the challenges and pitfalls of the gay scene, and the problems of work and family. "An extremely impressive performance" (*Christopher Street*).
ISBN 0 85449 130 9   *UK £9.95 ex-US AUS $19.95*

Christopher Bram
HOLD TIGHT
An erotic suspense novel that captures the feel of New York in the forties, the intensity of a nation at war, and the passion of men for their country and each other. "The author of *Surprising Myself* continues to break new ground with this spy thriller about Nazi interracial romance in a homosexual brothel" *(Kirkus Reviews).*
ISBN 0 85449 132 5   *UK £8.95 ex-US AUS $19.95*

The Gay Men's Press Collection

John Valentine
PUPPIES
Fall 1970 saw John Valentinue writing for a fragile underground paper in downtown Hollywood. A decaying cardborad building housed its seedy premises, and short of anywhere else to live he made his home in the rear office. "The building was the streetkids' social and community center... It was a sexual paradise".
"Puppies is fun reading" — Allen Ginsberg
ISBN 0 85449 258 5   *UK £7.95 US $12.95 AUS $17.95*

Mike Seabrook
OUT OF BOUNDS
When handsome 17-year-old Stephen Hill joined the cricket club, it was only a matter of time before young schoolmaster Graham Curtis fell head over heels in love. Mike Seabrook continues to explore the conflicts and rewards of gay life in a male environment.
ISBN 0 85449 177 5
UK £8.95 US $14.95 AUS $19.95

Mike Seabrook
UNNATURAL RELATIONS
This gripping yet tender story of two young people facing together a brutal assault on their human rights highlights the iniquitous position of gay teenagers under English law.
"I loved the book" — Jilly Cooper
ISBN 0 85449 116 3   *UK £8.95 US $14.95 AUS $19.95*

Send for our free catalogue to GMP Publishers Ltd,
P O Box 247, Swaffham, Norfolk PE37 8PA, England

Gay Men's Press books can be ordered from any bookshop in the
UK, North America and Australia, and from
specialised bookshops elsewhere.

Our distributors whose addresses are given in the front pages of
this book can also supply individual customers by mail order.
Send retail price as given plus 10% for postage and packing.

*For payment by Mastercard/American Express/Visa, please give
number, expiry date and signature.*

_____

_____

Name and address in block letters please:

Name
_____

Address
_____

_____

_____